Long Winters North

David Kenny

Long Winters North

Vanguard Press

VANGUARD PAPERBACK

© Copyright 2024
David Kenny

A CIP catalogue record for this title is
available from the British Library.

ISBN 978 1 83794 094 3

*Vanguard Press is an imprint of
Pegasus Elliot Mackenzie Publishers Ltd.*
www.pegasuspublishers.com

First Published in 2024

**Vanguard Press
Sheraton House Castle Park
Cambridge England**

Printed & Bound in Great Britain

FOR THE WILD AND FREE
UPPER PENINSULA OF MICHIGAN

CHAPTER 1

As the snowstorm moved in, quickly enveloping the lakeshore cabins and pine trees, a shadowy figure crouched low, cupping a left hand around a cigarette lighter and flicking the wheel with the right. A small flame sputtered and almost went out, but not before the flame touched the ground.

The fire spread quickly, racing along a narrow trail of doused fuel toward the nearby car. The sedan, soaked with gasoline from front to back, underneath, and all over the ground, burst into flames.

Seconds later, the car's gas tank explodes, a front door flies off, and the massive eruption shoots flames high above and into the pine trees.

Phil Sinclair had been singing along to his radio music in the Department of Natural Resources truck after checking on snowmobile conditions. He had just pulled into the front of the only gas station in the town of Paradise when his truck shuddered from the explosion. He screeches to a stop and jumps out. The intense smell of gasoline hits him in a repulsive wave. He looks around, wide-eyed, the blowing snow stinging his eyes. Then he looks up to see flames dancing in the night sky, covering the tops of nearby trees. Now he hears the low grumble of metal cracking and popping.

He runs around the corner of the station. A half block away, he can see the car in flames and even feel the heat on his snow-wet face. Phil wipes away the snow from his face and focuses intently on what he thought was a body in the burning car. He rushes back to the front of the station. He knew that Donna Merkle, the attendant, would be inside. But Donna was getting on in years and couldn't hear well.

Sure enough, Donna was there, watching a closed caption rerun of *Cheers*. The vibration of the sedan explosion, though, had caused her to get off her stool and look out the back window, but she could see nothing but black smoke.

"Donna!" he yelled. "I need to use your phone!"

"Oh dear, what was that? It sounded like a house blew up," Donna asks frantically.

"I need to use your phone. We need to get someone out here right now. The woods are on fire from a car exploding behind the gas station, and someone might be in it."

"Lock up when you're done. I'm not staying in here." Donna slides over a landline phone, grabs her purse, and throws the keys over to Phil across the counter.

"Pick up, pick up, pick up," Phil says to himself, dialing 911 and hearing another loud explosion from outside.

CHAPTER 2

A cell phone ringing breaks the silence of a cold winter night and the warm crackles of the fireplace in the cabin. In the cabin, a man is fast asleep in bed, covered head to toe by his flannel blanket, trying to ignore the never-ending ringing of his cell phone on a nightstand. Eventually, he reaches over and mutes the cell phone, letting out a frustrated grunt before turning over and sleeping again.

Within seconds, the phone begins to buzz again. As his patience runs out, he places the pillow over his head to drown out the noise from under his phone.

"Newberry is closed, so it will have to wait until morning," the man yells from under his pillow.

He exhales in relief when the phone stops buzzing.

On the end table, the phone buzzes again a few moments later.

Throwing off his blanket and picking up the phone, the man grunts after accidentally knocking over the beer on the floor.

Sitting on his bed, he grabs his phone and waits for the other end of the line to say something, but nothing happens.

With a sigh, he began to pull the phone away, ready to dismiss the call as a wrong number. But a loud voice echoed from the speaker.

"Bob, thank God you picked up. This is Phil Sinclair; I watch over the trails for the DNR up in Paradise. Are you able to hear me?" Phil asks.

"Yeah, barely."

"I'm in Paradise; you need to get up here right now if you can."

"I've had one too many Two Hearted Ales, Phil, to get out right now," says Bob, taking a few aspirins and drinking the rest of the beer he had knocked over.

Frustration laced Phil's voice as he rasped into the phone. "I've called everyone, but you're the only one who picks up. I know you're retired and not the Sheriff anymore, but the state cops are tied up. The blizzard's caused a monstrous pile-up on the highway to Saint Ignace. The operator said you were our only shot for help with the fire up here." A tremor of nerves ran through his voice, starkly contrasting the urgency that had propelled him to call.

"A fire in this mess? Isn't it a snowstorm up your way?" Bob says, staring out his window at heavy snow falling.

"As I pulled in to get gas, a car exploded behind the gas station, catching trees on fire around it. I'm not trained for car explosions; I just check on trails. The fire was too strong, so I couldn't get close enough, but I think someone is in the car, but I'm not sure."

Holding the phone in silence, Bob doesn't respond.

"Bob, are you still there?" Phil asks frantically.

"I'm still here, Phil," Bob says, putting on his Carhartt snow pants and a heavy winter jacket while holding the phone up to his ear with his shoulder. "I'll get in my plow truck and head up your way now. Don't leave; it might take me a while to get to you in this weather, but I'm on my way."

Bob throws on his hat and walks out of his cabin into the storm towards his plow truck, cleaning it off the best he can to drive north to Paradise to see first-hand what's happening.

It would usually be an easy thirty-five-minute drive any other time, but weather conditions this time meant Bob took over an hour with the heavy snowfall. The falling snow makes even his plow truck travel less than thirty-five miles per hour for most of the drive north.

The wind howled like a banshee, each gusts a battering ram against Bob's truck. Visibility plunged with every snowflake that clung to the windshield. The rumble strips, his only lifeline to the road, thrummed a frantic rhythm beneath his tires. Squinting through the whiteout, Bob finally spotted a faint shape against the swirling snow. It was the village limits sign for Paradise.

The world outside his windshield had been a chaotic ballet of swirling snow and howling wind. But as he crossed the threshold into Paradise, the storm abruptly surrendered. The snow thinned to a hesitant dusting, and the wind died to a sigh. As Bob nears the Paradise gas station, black smoke surrounds his truck, and a strong whiff of gasoline comes through his truck vents. Bob looks up, seeing the fire still roaring. He turns toward the fire, past the gas station, into a massive snowdrift from the winds coming off Lake Superior just feet away from the road, blocking the road completely, making walking the only option. Bob backs up, pulls next to the gas station, and puts on his hazard lights. So maybe wherever Phil is, he might see the lights flashing off his truck.

Slogging through the knee-deep snow, Bob reached for his pocket and fumbled out his flashlight. With a click, he sliced a cone of light into the swirling blackness. The snow, thick and heavy, turned an unsettling shade of gray in its harsh glow. A sliver of unease wormed its way into his gut, following what's left of the footprints left behind by Phil, and heading towards the fire. As he walks closer to the fire, the smoke intensifies, making it hard to see. Bob looks down and notices Phil's tracks have come to a stop.

Walking toward the fire, Bob finally sees what's left of the car in flames, down to the seats and undercarriage, as a tire blows up in front of him. He steps back, stopping to catch his breath and unzipping his jacket to balance the rising heat levels. He puts his hand above his eyes to see, and he can make out that it's a car-sized vehicle on fire and can see what's left of not one but two corpses burned down to the bones. Bob reaches into his coat pocket, taking out his phone to take pictures of what's left of the sedan and the bodies inside. As Bob is concentrating on taking pictures, a hand touches his shoulder. Bob jumps backward quickly, pulling out his pistol from his holster and dropping into a shooting position. The man who touched him throws his hands up in the air. Bob notices the DNR logo on the sleeve, realizing he almost shot Phil Sinclair.

"I almost unloaded a round in you, Phil!" Bob screamed in the strong winds.

"I tried to get your attention by yelling your way as I walked towards you, but the fire and winds are so loud," Phil yells to Bob, with only a few feet separating them.

"Follow me," Phil says, directing Bob.

Following Phil towards the car, Bob keeps his distance from the vehicle, as the sedan could explode again at any time, and the heat intensifies. Slowly, Phil and Bob walk towards the vehicle from the side, revealing more of the two bodies with limbs blown off from the heat, lying close to the sedan. Bob takes out his phone to take more photos and notices when zooming in a third burnt corpse in the back seat.

Running over to a tree and leaning over, Phil throws up from the trauma of seeing the burnt bodies.

"Are you all right, Phil?" Bob yells, walks over, and puts his hand on Phil's back.

"I'll make it," Phil says and signals with a thumbs up, slowly standing back up with Bob's help after throwing up and wiping his mouth off.

As Bob consults Phil, he notices a ring lying in the snow to his right next to a tree and takes out his phone to get a photo of the only evidence found that was not destroyed in the car fire.

"Let's get you inside somewhere; I'm going to make a call," Bob says to Phil, making a phone call gesture.

After helping Phil back to his truck, Bob quickly gets out of the wind and into his truck, grabs his phone from his jacket pocket, and makes a call.

"Come on, pick up, Bill," Bob says urgently.

"Bob, it's three a.m.! What in the world is going on?" Bill asks.

"I can't explain it all right now, Bill, but you know I wouldn't bother you unless this was an emergency. You need to get up to Paradise now with your fire truck," Bob says. "We have a car on fire in Paradise with people in it."

"People in it? On fire?" Bill asks.

"Well, what's left of them is on fire. The bodies are burned down to the bones. I've never seen anything like this."

Silence.

"On my way," Bill responds.

CHAPTER 3

7 Years Earlier

Kansas City
Bucca Di Peppo at The Country Club Plaza
Friday Night.

A grin stretched across the face of the young man with short brown hair. "We deserve dessert, right?" he said, his eyes twinkling playfully at the youthful blonde woman across the table. "Yes, we do. Let's split a main course, so I don't feel bad about having it."

"I'm so glad it's the weekend, Joy. I'm not built for the nine-to-five corporate world."

"You've got to find that one thing, Willis. Something you enjoy that doesn't feel like work, like my dad's experience with his sawmill. How about getting back into being a reporter? You have a wall of journalism awards for your stories from the college paper and the years of writing and researching with your parents' local newspaper." Joy replies

"The love for investigative journalism died when my father passed away."

"You can't run away from it forever. Once a journalist, always a journalist, or at least that's what they say in communication classes."

"I can make a good cup of coffee."

"Now that's something I could see you doing the rest of your life. Look at all the coffee shops popping up around town; it seems like one's on every corner. "With your baking skills, Joy, we could make something special if we wanted to," Willis responds with excitement.

"My dad always says my hometown, Newberry, needs a good bakery and coffee shop."

"But we have a great life here; there's no reason to move. Kansas City's a thriving area. Isn't your hometown like a thousand people and shrinking by the day?" Willis asks.

"Newberry may be a small town, but it's special to thousands, including me. In the summer, the area gets so much tourist traffic. Once we finally make a trip up north, you will understand, trust me. Whitecap waves make their way to the shores, crashing on the miles of sand-covered beaches with an endless view of the lake, feeling more like a saltless ocean, but even better," Joy says excitedly to Willis. "Miles upon miles of shorelines filled with rocks like you've never seen, driftwood, and crystal-clear water that sometimes looks like the Caribbean. Also, don't get me started on the giant pines. Oh, how I miss those right now. I can almost smell them. The waters feel endless when looking out across Lake Superior. The largest freshwater lake in the world."

"I can't wait to see how this place lives up to your stories."

"I promise, I'm not making this up," Joy says.

"You light up when you talk about Michigan."

"It's the northern girl in my blood. I love the Mitten State, but I'm talking about up north past the Mackinac Bridge, in the wild pine-covered woods, the one and only God's country," Joy says.

"God's country? No matter how amazing a smile you make at me, God's country is the Ozarks in Missouri. Or at least it was to me until it became too hard on my mother to go back to the lake after my dad passed away two years ago. Every summer, my whole family would take a week off from running the newspaper and go camping in the Ozarks by Osage Beach. The Ozarks can't be beat in the summer. Riding around those lakes in a pontoon and looking up at the sunset, overlooking the hills reflecting on the lake around you that's my God's country. Even all the little gift shops have a section of God's country mugs and wooden signs for your cabin. I guess there are many areas that call themselves God's countries; we each get our own."

"The Ozarks are nice, but I promise you, no matter how good your childhood memories are, they don't compare to the one true God's country, and that's the Upper Peninsula of Michigan."

"You're not giving up, are you?" Willis asks, chuckling.

"Nope, you're never going to win this one. I betcha, I will convince you."

"Well, when we visit up north, you will have one shot to convince me, as I'm pretty convinced it's the Ozarks. By the way, your northern accent jumps out when you start talking about home."

"No, it doesn't," Joy responds, with a muffled giggle that vibrates through her hands

"It does too. I even heard you say 'betcha' this time. You being a northern girl is one of the hundreds of reasons I fell in love with you," Willis tells Joy, making her blush even more.

"I hope you love it when you visit. You can't beat the summers in the Upper Peninsula, but I have to be honest, the smell of the wood stove in the winter is my favorite time of year," Joy says, taking a drink.

As Willis and Joy finish their meal, Joy's phone rings next to her setting on the side of the table.

"Should I pick up? It's my mom; if I don't pick up, she'll instantly think I was kidnapped," Joy asks Willis.

"It's your mom. You know she won't stop calling if you don't pick up, and it will be fun to catch up for a minute and see what's going on. I haven't heard much since they came down for our wedding last month."

Willis sits back and watches Joy talk on the phone across the table, picking up parts of the conversation but more enjoying seeing his wife catch up with family.

"My mom wants to see if we can come for a visit for Thanksgiving. Do you think we can get the time off?" Joy asks, smiling at Willis, hoping for a yes response from him.

"Tell her we will do all we can to make it happen, so yes. We can put in our time off request on Monday before everyone else puts in for November," Willis says.

"He said yes, Mom. I'll call you after we get time off from work. I can't wait to see you, Dad, everybody."

"Love you, Ruth!" Willis shouts across the table to Joy's mom on the other end of the phone.

"It's really happening," Joy says, clapping her hands in excitement.

CHAPTER 4

"Here we go; now's your chance to prove Michigan is as special as you've said for the last year and a half. This is my first adventure to the Great White North and Lake Superior. The first leg of the trip from Kansas City to Chicago went smoothly, so here's hoping this flight is the same," Willis says, tightening his seatbelt on the plane and looking over at Joy with excitement.

"I hope you fall in love with my home. I've built the Upper Peninsula up, haven't I?" Joy asks nervously.

"You're a natural-born saleswoman."

Joy reaches down and pulls out a small roadside map she placed in her purse of Michigan that her dad had sent her. A habit she picked up from her dad's love for the atlas and road maps.

"Look right here," Joy says, pointing at the road map to a town called Marquette. "Ever heard of the city where we're heading, Marquette, before our flight?" Joy asks.

"Only what you've told me about. That looks pretty far away from Newberry. Is that the closest airport?" Willis asks.

"In the Upper Peninsula of Michigan, we measure things by hours instead of minutes. Newberry's about one hour from any other town; the same goes for other towns up north. So, to me, it's not far at all, only two and a half hours away," Joy says. "The closest big box store like Walmart is seventy miles away from Newberry."

"Two and a half hours is the closest airport?" Willis says, shaking his head in disbelief.

"No, we have a small airport in Newberry for personal planes and another one just over an hour away in Sault Ste. Marie, but that airport hardly has any flights unless you jump across to the Canadian side in Ontario. My parents stopped going over to Canada when you had to start using a passport after 9/11. My dad mentioned to me that he has so many stories he wants to tell you on the drive back to Newberry."

"Today's flight will be one hour and forty-five minutes. If you are lucky enough to have a window seat, you are in for a treat today. Enjoy the clear skies and the views over Lake Michigan and the Chicago skyline on our way to Marquette. The flight could get a little turbulent as we hit weather farther north, so please stay buckled in and enjoy your flight," the pilot says over the intercom.

"My favorite lake is Lake Superior, but Lake Michigan is a close second," Joy says in her seat as the flight takes off, holding Willis's hand tightly.

"Oh, look, Willis, Sears Tower!" Joy says as Willis leans close and stares out the window at the remarkable view of the Chicago skyline and Lake Michigan.

"I never expected Lake Michigan to be this big; it looks like the ocean."

"See, I told you," Joy says as she hits his arm softly, laughing.

During the flight, Joy spent forty-five minutes pointing out places outside the window until the view became cloud-covered. Joy stays glued to the window, hoping for a break in the cloud cover so she can keep sharing past adventures in Wisconsin until they reach Michigan.

"Look, Willis, snow!" Joy says with excitement over to Willis, relaxing in his seat. "It's hard to tell how far north we are, but I guess we must be a little north of Green Bay right now. Look at how beautiful the change is from green fields to snow-covered land. Even the lake has a little ice buildup. It must be a colder fall," Joy shares as Willis looks over her shoulder at the lake ice below.

The skies stay clear as Willis and Joy get closer to the airport in Marquette. Joy holds Willis's hand tightly as they come in for the landing. The pilot wishes everyone a safe adventure in Marquette as everyone leaves the plane.

As Joy and Willis exit the arrival area into the main terminal, Joy's mother, Ruth, greets them with big bear hugs, and Joy's father, Ted, gives Willis a big handshake and welcoming smile.

"Warmest welcome to God's country," Ted says. "Let's get you to Newberry. If you are hungry, we can stop at Pizza Hut before leaving town."

"No need for that. I made some delicious fresh pasties for Willis and Joy to enjoy on the drive home," Ruth says.

"A true Michigan meal, all the way back to the first logging camps," Ted says.

Ted shares stories about Bigfoot experiences and logging deliveries across the Upper Peninsula. His stories keep Willis alert during the long drive back to Newberry, surrounded by swamps and pines, driving straight as an arrow as the daylight starts to fade.

"Bored yet, Willis?" Ruth sarcastically asks from the back seat.

"Not at all; it's so different here; your trees are massive and this area has so much more snow," Willis says, looking out his window as the snow-covered pines cover both sides of the road, like driving through a tunnel of trees.

"I'm bored," Ruth chuckles. "You never get used to these long drives; you just tough it out. How did you like the pastie?"

"It was delicious. I'm glad you told me what's in it first, as it looked like a pizza calzone, so the taste of potatoes and onions would've been a shocker for sure," Willis says.

"I'm so glad you liked it. Some like it better with ketchup, which I brought just in case, but I like it best just the way it is," Ruth says.

As Ted continued driving down the remote, long stretch of M-28 known as the Seney Stretch, Willis looked around, with only woods and marshland for the entire forty-mile stretch as daylight quickly faded. "It might be swampland, but this is God's country," Ted said. "Around here, it's just you and the road. And maybe a moose or two."

After making it through the Seney Stretch, Willis sees a road sign half-covered with blowing snow, saying 'Newberry, twelve miles'. Like a switch, the weather changes drastically, from a star-filled, clear sky with a full moon to clouds covering the moon above, bringing snow with them.

Willis comments on the heavy snow, but Ted continues driving unfazed.

"Ah, this ain't nothing but a little lake effect. I'll just stick to my standard of fifty miles per hour, what I call the perfect speed for any kind of travel," Ted says confidently.

"I can't even tell if we are still on the road," Willis says, looking out the front of the van.

"Oh, you would know it," Ruth says from behind.

"Look, you can see the turn for Newberry up ahead at that blinking light," Ted says, pointing ahead.

"If I get too far over the rumble strips on the right, the strips will give me a little rumble, and the road will let me know," Ted says calmly as he turns at the blinking light into Newberry.

Willis looks on as the snow calms as they reach a *Welcome to Newberry, the gateway to the Falls* billboard out his window. Then the streetlights build, lighting up the tops of the massive snow-covered, beautiful pines as they drive into town.

"Newberry mostly shuts up shop for the night around eight p.m. on a late night. You can see most businesses are already asleep for the night. It's so peaceful in town this time of year without the summer traffic," Ted shares.

"You've already got more snow than we get back in Kansas City all year."

"This is just the start; before long, the snow banks might get as tall as you and me," Ted says.

"What's that up ahead with all the lights? Is that the hospital or a shopping mall?" Willis asks.

"That right there, Willis, is the Newberry prison. The prison was a city within a village originally called the Newberry State Hospital for the Insane. My mother used to work there. I'll have to drive you in front of the old state hospital section when the weather calms," Ted says.

Ted points around at different places, telling stories, but it's still snowing heavily outside, so Willis acts like he can see what Ted's talking about until the van eventually turns down a long driveway.

"We're home," Joy says. Looking ahead, she sees home with the kitchen light on and smoke coming from the chimney.

Willis and Ted grab the luggage and the women head inside. Ted points to his house, describing how his father built the home after moving to Newberry from Finland. Within seconds of walking through the front door, the chill is replaced with the warmth and smell of firewood from the wood stove filling Joy's childhood home. The wood stove quickly heats the house, making it feel like a sauna.

Willis sits at the dining room table while Ruth takes a large baking sheet out of the oven. On the sheet are giant cinnamon rolls that are so big they almost fall over the edge of the pan.

As Ted finishes his second roll, he turns around, digs into a metal filing cabinet filled with papers, and takes out a road map. Ted goes over Willis and Joy's trip to Newberry from Kansas City, showing different places he loved to visit on the drive, and then shows Willis locations of land he owned that he wanted to take Joy and Willis to tomorrow. After a long day of traveling, they all went upstairs to get a well-deserved rest.

CHAPTER 5

The following day, Willis smells the firewood, maple syrup, and fresh coffee coming from downstairs.

"If anyone's hungry, breakfast is ready," Ruth yells from downstairs in the kitchen.

Willis and Joy walk downstairs to a large breakfast spread across the dining room table, enough to feed ten.

"Look outside; the snow has stopped, just blue skies in every direction. I will take the rest of the day off cutting timber, so I can show you around. Let's go up to the Tahquamenon Falls," Ted says.

"You're going to love the falls," Joy says to Willis while covering her blueberry pancakes with maple syrup.

Willis, Joy, and her parents load into Ted's van and head out of town towards Tahquamenon Falls. During the thirty-minute drive north, Ted shared stories about the old logging camps that once occupied this area. He also explained how Newberry built the village by the railroad instead of following the trend of other cities in the Upper Peninsula, which built their towns by the water. As Ted continues storytelling, Willis wonders if it takes thirty minutes to drive to Tahquamenon Falls or if Ruth is right that it's Ted's slow driving. Ted shares stories about the Tahquamenon Falls area and how Luce County is proud to be the largest school district east of the Mississippi River in area size, of course, not population, with kids sometimes riding over an hour on the bus ride to and from school every day.

"We're here; you may not see the Tahquamenon Falls yet, but I bet you'll hear them thundering when you open your door," Ted tells Willis as they turn into the Tahquamenon State Park.

Willis exited the van, hearing the rushing sound of the falls in the distance and noticing the higher snow levels than back in Newberry. After switching into snow boots, they walked towards the sound of the waterfall, following the trail of foot tracks.

"There's something special or mysterious about hearing something before you see it. Listen to the power of that rushing water." Ted shares with Willis. Joy holds Willis's hand tightly as they follow the footprints of others in the deep snow, catching brief views of the massive waterfall between the thick pine tree lines. The powerful sound of water falling over the edge and a mist growing more prominent as they walk closer and closer. The pines clear as they finish the walk down the wooden steps to the viewing deck as the wide river flows like a painting downstream to the golden roaring waters, separating the snowcapped evergreens on both sides.

Willis glanced at Joy, both standing close to the railing, relishing the mist from the waterfall soaking them.

"I get it now. I understand all of it. You win," Willis says.

"Understand what?" Joy asks while still looking at the roaring waterfall in front of her.

"This *is* God's country," Willis responds, taking in the view in front of him and realizing just how right Joy was all along.

CHAPTER 6

Six years later
New Year's Eve night, Newberry, Michigan

A moving truck slowly drives down Newberry's quiet, snow-covered main street as the cold winter sun slips away. The truck drives under the Christmas lights, turning on for the evening, right before the truck drives under the lights like a welcoming sign. The moving truck pulls into an alleyway right next to a large three-story brick building towering over the other buildings around it, coming to a stop. After the truck comes to a complete stop, a padlock jingles on the back of the movie truck as someone tries to wrestle with the lock being stuck. After unlocking the large steel rear door, it's pulled open, quickly rising, revealing a cold Willis standing in a heavy winter jacket and blue beanie, looking up at all his belongings.

"Where to start? Willis says to himself, rubbing his hands together to warm up while looking into the packed moving truck.

"My dad must be smiling as wide as Lake Superior right now, knowing we will bring life back to The Newberry Building. I'm glad the old owners took our offer. My dad loved watching over the building till we could get here," Joy says to Willis while unbuckling a young boy from his car seat in the moving truck and putting him into her arms.

"I don't know how we managed to pull this off, but we did. It was time for a change from Kansas City, and there was no better place to do it than in your hometown. The deal we got at this building also helped. We would've never been able to afford a place like this in KC," Willis says to Joy as he looks over at the old brick building and takes in a glimpse of the boarded-up businesses across the road.

"What's the temperature out anyway?" Willis asks.

"Two degrees and dropping. I have Archer bundled up; he'll love playing in all this snow," Joy responded, standing next to Willis with their son in her arms.

"Seriously, two degrees?" Willis responds, shocked by how cold it is.

"Negative seven out with the wind chill; welcome to winter up north," Joy says, patting Willis on the back.

"While I have a minute, I want to look in the front windows while we wait for your parents and the keys. It's been years since I stepped foot in this place. The pictures we were sent helped with buying sight unseen, but I would love to take a quick look around the property to see what we need to fix first."

Willis walks over to the front of the Newberry Building. "I bet you have some stories to tell," Willis says, touching the brick wall and looking up at his new building, traversing slowly through the snow to his new building's front door. Willis wipes away frost on a front window and looks in the window, revealing a large, empty, dark room that used to be a dive bar. As he walks further down the front of the Newberry Building to try to get a better view from another window, Willis notices a bright yellow paper taped to one of the front doors. He goes over to read it and sees a picture of a man, looking to be around his age, with a large, bold print above it saying, *Help us find who killed Tim Dawson.*

"My parents are here." Joy yells from the back of the building as Willis reads over the flier.

"I'll be right there," Willis replies as he takes down the missing person flier and folds it up, putting it into his front jacket pocket, before heading back to greet Ted and Ruth.

"You made it in one piece," Ruth says with excitement.

"This old gem of a building is in pristine shape. They sure built things better back in those days. With some hard work, we should have this place sparkling again in no time, like it did in the 1910s. I've checked on the Newberry Building every day since you bought it. The building has held up better in the winter than my house. Look at how big my grandson is getting; I can't believe he's already three." Ted says as he picks up his grandson.

"Well, what are we doing out here, freezing? Let's get inside," Ruth says, heading toward the front of the building.

Ted handed Willis the keys as they reached the front door. They all entered, and the green-painted copper tin ceiling caught Willis's eye as he flipped on the lights in the room. "That wallpaper will be the first thing to go," Joy says, looking at the vintage, ripped purple wallpaper.

"This building holds so much history; if only these walls could talk," Ted says.

"I bet you wouldn't want to hear most of them," Ruth says.

"You might be right," Willis replies.

Creaking floorboards accompanied their slow ascent as Willis and the others followed Ted up the aged wooden steps.

They reached the third floor, a labyrinth of doorways leading to unknown rooms. Some doorways revealed faded carpets, while others gaped open, exposing bare floorboards and chipped plaster. Ted leaned against a cast-iron bed frame, its ornate design a stark contrast to the room's neglect.

"This floor had a name back in the day," Ted said, his voice dropping to a conspiratorial whisper. "Divorcee Row. It seems a lot of fellas ended up here after a bit too much drink or a wandering eye. Temporary digs until things blow over at home, you see."

Willis points out the different layers of wallpaper, shocked by the lack of effort in removing the old wallpaper. Joy ran her hand along the fabric wallpaper. A pungent aroma, a telltale blend of tobacco and cigar smoke, wafted up from the decades-old residue trapped within. With a grimace, she stepped back from the wall.

After looking around the building, Willis realizes they still have a truck to empty, a task waiting on him. Willis walks down the large wooden Victorian staircase that leads down to the main floor. As he steps outside, the local drivers slowly drive by, waving to him, wondering what's finally happening with the Newberry Building and who the new owners are.

"I guess we will soon be the talk of the town, won't we?" Willis asks Ted.

"News and rumors spread fast around Newberry; you and Joy are already the talk of the town. It's impossible to believe most of what you hear in this small village. The best way to get the truth is to grab a copy of our weekly paper, *The Newberry News*. The paper does a great job. Willis, you won't find deep-dive journalism like you did in the *Kansas City Star*, but I think you'll still enjoy the weekly read. Maybe you could write a column sharing your journalistic experience with Newberry once you're all situated," Ted says as he joins Willis outside to help unload the moving truck.

Willis sighed, watching another car slow down in front of the house. "Starting to feel like a spectacle," he muttered. "I have seen that car a couple of times already, and some folks even pulled out their cameras. People must think we're nuts for moving in during the winter months."

Under the street lights, a lady pulling her groceries on a child's sled behind her across the street walked in their direction as Willis and the family continued unloading their belongings. The lady stops as she reaches the moving truck and asks, "So you are the ones who bought the Newberry Building? I'm glad someone is finally brave enough to buy it, but beware, that place is haunted. A ghost scared off the old owners. You know that place is haunted, don't you? I see those ghosts all the time from my boyfriend's apartment across the street from above the insurance offices. Crazy things happen in that building and all around this village. I wouldn't bring a child into that building if it were me. Since that building closed months ago, people have started to disappear more often in this town." The woman says with a serious stare.

"I don't believe in ghosts myself, but if I'm wrong, I'm sure they're just looking for a conversation. Thanks for the warning." Willis responds kindly to the lady with a smile.

The lady just looks straight in silence at Willis after his comments and then looks away, walking on with her sled, loaded with groceries, behind her.

"I can tell you for certain that there's no ghost in these walls. I've been checking the place for the last couple of months. People are a unique breed around here sometimes. Some may have been released after the Newberry State Hospital closed years ago, or they might be the kids of those folks. That lady sure seemed like one of those former state hospital patients," Ted says to Willis with a grin.

"So, there are more like her around town?" Willis asks.

"A couple of handfuls of them, I would guess. Willis, you will find some of the most loving people in the world living up here with giant hearts that would do anything for you. Then there are some of the most broken, trying to escape from the world or, even worse, trying to take it out on others. I've heard that sometimes people move up here because it's so easy to live off the government, being so limited to employment. A person, I believe, should have to work for a living. Do something; make a difference in this world. After I wrapped up my time serving our country in the Marines, all I could do was think about getting back home and working in the woods," Ted says to Willis as they walk over to the moving truck and pick up a couch to take inside.

"My dad was a marksman in the Marine Corps," Joy says, walking by and overhearing their conversation.

"Oh, by the way, before I forget, I want to show you two things in the basement," Ted says to Joy and Willis, piquing their interest in what he found.

Joy and Willis follow Ted towards the basement, curious about what he's found, passing by Ruth and Archer on their way.

"Mom, do you want to come down to the basement with us?" Joy asks Ruth.

"That basement? It can stay a mystery. My feet won't be setting foot on those stairs, no matter the price. Any time your dad checks on the building, this is as far as I'll ever go," Ruth says hesitantly.

Ted reaches up, pulling a chain for the staircase lights as they walk down to the basement, leaving Ruth behind upstairs.

"I can do this; it's better to be with you than be left behind up here," Ruth says nervously, gaining the courage to slowly walk down with her hands on the wall.

Ted guides everyone around the basement, showing the different areas turning on lights as they walk into a new room, from the boiler room to the maid's cleaning area to the old phone control switch area that ran the phone calls around Newberry at one time. Ted shares how the lady phone operators switched the connection lines and were known to listen in on interesting conversations. Stopping in a center hallway, he asks Joy to turn off the lights in the room behind her.

"Alright, alright, Ted, I get it! The dark basement is definitely spooky. Can we turn the lights back on now?" Ruth asked while thinking about rushing upstairs.

"That would've been a great plan, but this is why." Ted turns his flashlight on and points it downward, asking everyone to step back as he lowers down with the flashlight, revealing a compass carved into the floor beneath them.

"When they built this building, the size of the building was so big, workers would get confused down here on what way they were heading, so they added the floor compass to help them find their way," Ted says.

"Smart. I could see that compass coming in handy with all these turns down here," Willis says, looking at the directional compass on the basement floor.

"One thing even better is yet to come. Follow me," Ted says, walking everyone into another room he called the old bridal suite, now filled with debris left over tools and unfinished walls, looking left behind in the beginning stages of an unfinished remodel. Ted walks over to the basement foundation wall and leans down, revealing a hole in the original brick wall with old, broken beer bottles lying near it.

"Can anyone tell me why this large basement would have a large hole in the bottom of the wall? " Ted asks.

"I would say that hole was a spot where underage drinkers would hide their drinks," Willis says.

"This isn't just bottles and a hole in the wall, Willis; this is a tunnel from the Prohibition era running from here all the way across the street to the Masonic Temple. They probably used this tunnel for years, passing illegal booze back and forth across it, but after decades of road work above it, the tunnel looks like it caved in some time ago."

After taking a tour of the basement and Ted's finds, Willis stops for a minute alone as everyone heads upstairs and back outside to help bring in some more items from the moving truck, looking around the empty room and soaking in what journey lies ahead.

CHAPTER 7

Weeks passed after the move from Kansas City to Newberry, with the grand opening rapidly approaching for Willis and Joy's brand-new bakery, The Northern Bites. Endless hours of painting and remodeling projects are almost complete. Still, with more money than expected paid for unexpected leaks and broken equipment and no money left, Willis feels uncertain about how to finish the last major projects.

"Praying this is the last leak we find," Willis says, exhausted, wiping his forehead.

"How much is left in the budget?" Joy asks.

"What budget? After fixing that last leak, we are on credit cards to finish these last projects, unless we borrow some from your parents or ask mine, but I would hate to do that. We are so close to opening and having money rolling in." Willis replies.

"I hope it rolls in," Joy says.

"It will. These doors will open on March 1st. I promise," Willis says to Joy as they work together, putting some sinks in the bakery.

"Do you know what you're doing, by the way?" Joy asks nervously.

"The YouTube videos made it look simple. I feel pretty confident about it. The handyman on the video said you need to pull these bolts tight right here," Willis says with a grunt as he tightens the nut a bit too tight, busting the line and making the water line leak all over the newly installed floor.

"What did you do? Turn off the water!" Joy screamed, getting soaked by the water leaks and trying to cover her face.

"I must've put too much muscle into it, I guess. At least it's just water," Willis says, looking at Joy, trying to make her smile but not getting anywhere.

"That's not just water; it's money and time we don't have. The list is getting long; we need to hire someone who will do it right. Maybe we can put something up at the grocery stores and gas stations. I noticed a lot of pull tabs torn off the ads."

"I tried calling all the contacts from the handyman list we got from your dad, which was a shortlist, but either no one is working in the offseason, they retired, or the handymen are charging insane amounts for the work. You would think people would be begging for projects in the winter, not overcharging," Willis says.

"I'm grateful for all the unexpected help from friends and family, but we're at the point now where we can't just rely on free help and need some professional help to finish this, no matter the price. The opening is just three weeks away. Look outside at the old awnings flipping back and forth in the winds, half-broken off. That's a lawsuit waiting to happen with the next big storm, blowing them off," Joy says, staring out the window at the large, ripped awning running the entire front of the Newberry Building.

"I can't stand that awning. I wish I could take it down now, but I'll have to wait until late spring when the weather is better. It's -12 degrees outside, and the snow banks are at least five feet high. It will take someone who is crazy to get those awnings down before we open," Willis says.

"The baking mission begins in the kitchen. First things first, I need to test all the appliances and ensure they're in top baking condition," Joy says, standing up, wiping off her hands with a rag.

"Look how far we've come, right? It's really coming together." Willis leaned in for a kiss, a hopeful glint in his eyes. But before his lips could touch hers, Joy's finger gently blocked his path. The playful gesture hung heavy in the air, leaving Willis waiting.

Joy tilted her head up, holding Willis's attention. "Listen," she said, her voice firm but soft. "Find a plumber tonight, then, and only then, do you get this." She gestured towards his lips with a playful wink, a hint of challenge in her eyes.

"As soon as I clean up my mess, I won't come home till I find someone to help us," Willis responds.

Joy decides to give Willis a hand, grabbing a mop and bucket to clean up the mess on the soaked floor. Minutes after starting to mop, Willis and Joy hear the front door chime, and a young man with a short scruffy beard with only a dirty half-unbuttoned red flannel shirt, mud-covered jeans, and a stocking cap walks in, bringing the harsh breeze from the negative temperatures into the building and throwing out a cigarette before entering.

"Hi, sorry about just dropping in. I'm not a salesman; far from it. The name's Noah. My fiancée, Sarah, told me late last night, over at Zellar's Restaurant, that she heard you were looking for help on some projects around here," Noah says.

Willis and Joy look at each other in disbelief, knowing that just who they needed had walked through their front door.

"We are. I'm Willis, and this is Joy," Willis says, reaching out his hand and shaking Noah's.

"This place almost looks like a different place already. It sure needed it. I used to hang out in this dive bar when I was nineteen. This bar was the only place that would serve

36

you a beer underage at the time, saving us from having to drive over to Canada. Just getting that smoke smell out had to be a chore in this place," Noah says, looking around the room.

"So, what type of work do you do?" Joy asks.

"A little bit of anything and everything. I grew up helping my family's construction business in Engadine. Here's one of my cards. You can see on my business card that I can do a little bit of everything, and that's why I named my business Mr. Do It All. After years of working at badly run places, I got sick of dealing with other people's nonsense and seeing them taken advantage of, so I decided to forge my own path. It's been a slow start, but the more people see my work, the more I get. People also like my slogan, 'Don't cuss, call us'."

"I can understand the frustration of working for other people. That's one of the reasons we started this place," Willis says.

"So, what are you going to do with this place?" Noah asks, taking a look at one of the projects left unfinished on the walls.

"A bakery called Northern Bites at first, then we have plans for every inch of the building but want to take it one step at a time," Willis responds.

Willis and Joy walk Noah around the building, showing him all the projects that are still incomplete.

"Thanks for showing me around. I know you are busy. One of my company rules is that there is no upfront money until you see my work and approve it. I don't set prices; just what you can pay is good enough," Noah says.

"If you don't feel scared off by what we showed you, we would love to have you start as soon as you can," Willis says.

"Let me grab my coat from the house I just finished helping down the block, and I'll be right back. Some of their kids jammed toys down their toilet, backing the toilet up and flooding the place. I've been digging a trench all morning for their septic. When I get back here, I'll start ripping up that kitchen floor in the back like you wanted. Also, that old awning outside looks like the next snowstorm might rip it off your building. I always hated that awning. I want to get that awning down for you as soon as the weather will let me get up there," Noah says, looking up at the building's old awning, standing in the strong wind as he heads out the front door.

"Let me know anything you need," Willis says.

"See you in a couple of minutes," Noah says, shutting the front door.

"So, do I get that kiss now?" Willis says, walking towards Joy in the middle of the bakery after Noah left.

"Yes, you do. You're either a lucky man or God's watching out for us," Joy says, kissing Willis.

"Both," Willis says with a smile.

"Now, let's make sure Noah doesn't kill himself. Keep a watchful eye on him," Joy says.

CHAPTER 8

Days pass, and Noah's handyman skills speed up the finishing stages, allowing Willis to focus more on the business side and letting Joy perfect her baking. With two weeks to spare, as Willis hangs artwork in the bakery, Noah takes advantage of a good weather day to try to take down the massive awnings. As Willis works inside, he hears a large thump sound against the building, sounding like metal hitting against the brick exterior. Willis looks over and sees the scaffolding collapsing, crashing to the ground, and drops what he is doing, running outside to the door to check on Noah. Willis sees the fallen scaffolding in the massive pile in the snow, with no sign of Noah. Fearing Noah might be trapped and seriously hurt underneath, Willis starts pulling metal and boards away, but he doesn't find anyone under it. Over Willis's shoulder, he hears a faint grunt and turns around, noticing a boot sticking out of a snow bank and Noah slowly pushing his way up out of the snow.

"That jump must've knocked me out for a moment," Noah says, digging his way out slowly, shaking his head while lying in the snow.

"I thought the scaffolding crushed you. How many close calls have you had working on this building so far?" Willis asks, helping Noah back up to his feet.

"I have nine lives like a cat. If my life count is correct, I should at least have three lives left. On the bright side, at least the awning came down," Noah says with a laugh, looking at all the debris in the snow around him and Willis.

"I told you, those ghosts in your building don't want you around; they're going to try to kill you all," yells the lady from the move-in day who has been watching from her boyfriend's window across the street.

"That lady is crazy," Noah says, murmuring to Willis, fake smiling, and waving back at the lady.

"I bet she's one of those patients from the old insane ward at the state hospital that never left the area after it closed. So glad we got the curtains up to our rooms," Willis says to Noah quietly while waving up at the lady in the window.

"Everything is fine," Noah shouts back to the lady as she just stares back without responding. The lady closes her window and walks away.

"Noah, I need to pay you this for all this. You've more than earned this check," Willis says, reaching into his pocket and handing Noah a check. "I hope this is enough to cover your time and equipment."

"I'm used to getting pies or a thank you from old ladies around town, so this check is more than I expected. I appreciate you giving me a chance. I know some of my ways might be unorthodox, but I stand behind my work."

The next day, Noah and Willis finished the last projects inside together. Willis would help when Noah could use an extra hand to not fall to his death or to make sure nothing was damaged. While talking with Noah, Willis picks up some unique traits in Noah's accent, different from what he's heard in other Yooper accents in the area. One day, he decides to ask Noah about it.

"Hey, your U.P. accent is different. What part are you from originally?" Willis asks.

"I betcha it's the Amish left over from my childhood; I call it Yooperish. Growing up, I lived in an Amish community just south of Newberry towards Engadine, which I left when I turned seventeen. That was the best decision I've ever made, and I've never regretted it. I never seemed to fit in. There were too many rules for me, and I was always getting into trouble. It's difficult not to speak to my family anymore, but I had to leave. From time to time, my sister secretly contacts me. My first week out of the Amish community, I met my fiancé, Sarah. Despite breaking up a few times, we always ended up back together. I finally proposed over Christmas, and lucky for me, she said yes this time. Best day of my life," Noah says, finishing the nailing on a shelf in the bakery.

"I can't wait to meet Sarah. Why don't you bring her on opening day? Whatever you want is on me."

"Thanks; I wouldn't miss your opening day for the world," Noah replies.

After Noah has just completed the final shelf installation behind the checkout counter, while Willis takes a stroll around the bakery. As he looks around, Willis realizes the immense progress that has been made in the construction process. From the rotted wooden flooring to the outdated decor, Northern Bites now looks like the bakery Willis had always dreamed of. This transformation fills Willis with a sense of pride and accomplishment, as he feels that his business is finally ready for the world to see.

CHAPTER 9

A man hard asleep in bed suddenly wakes up, realizing he has overslept his alarm and is going to be late for work. He quickly splashes his face with water to help wake him up. Rushing out of his mobile home, the man hits his shoulder hard on the doorframe while trying to put on his jacket after frantically putting on his correctional officer's uniform, quickly turning around to grab his name badge and keys he almost forgot. After rushing to get ready, the correctional officer jumps into his pickup truck and pealing out of his driveway, rushing to work on the icy roads as sunset approaches.

A few minutes later, as the sun rises on the cold winter morning, the door to his mobile home opens, and someone wearing wet black snow boots walks inside, whistling in the tone only a man could make. The individual in dark gloves walks through the mobile home, slowly looking around, stopping by the living room couch. The man stops whistling as he reaches into his jacket and drops needles, pipes, and small plastic bags containing meth all over the couch and floor. After dropping the drugs, the man starts to whistle again as he walks over to the kitchen area, turning the oven on high with his gloves, then opening the oven door. Leaning down, the man cuts the propane line underneath the oven with a Swiss army knife, which starts to fill the room with gases.

As the person walks towards the front door of the mobile home to leave, the person stops, reaches into his jacket pocket, takes out a pack of cigarettes and a lighter, and puts the cigarette in his mouth and lights it. Then he reaches over with his arm to the couch at his left and drops the lit cigarette next to the staged needles and drugs, starting a small fire that grows quickly on the furniture. As the person walks out of the mobile home, he leaves the front door wide open behind him, with smoke building quickly as the person walks away. The farther the person walks away from the mobile home, the bigger the fire builds behind them, bursting out of the glass windows. The man continues to whistle, heading into the thick, dark forest close by, vanishing into the shadows as the mobile home goes up into a towering blaze. Within seconds, the mobile home catches fully on fire and explodes, blowing parts of the trailers all over the correctional officer's yard, destroying every last inch.

CHAPTER 10

An alarm goes off at five a.m., but Willis has been up for a while just lying, contemplating the day ahead for hours. Willis rolls out of bed, with Joy following shortly behind him, and walks over to Archer's bedroom.

"Here we go," Willis whispered over to Joy in her ear, then looked down at their son, still deeply asleep.

"Wow, that overnight low of -38 degrees was brutal! It might be a record. Not the record I wanted to break. It's time for me, I guess, to get downstairs and start the ovens; that should help heat the bakery up," Joy says.

Willis and Joy quietly head downstairs into the kitchen, turning on the lights in the Northern Bites kitchen.

"I wouldn't be going anywhere today if it were me. Do you hear those howling winds? I bet you can barely stand up outside right now," Willis says while helping Joy turn on the ovens in the kitchen.

"We have bills to pay, so let's hope you're wrong," Joy says. "Did you lock the back?" Joy asks, hearing the back door open.

"I did, I promise. I hope it's not some drunk breaking in after leaving Johnny's Bar down the block," Willis says, walking over to see who's at his back door cautiously.

"Wow, it smells amazing in here! I completely forgot you don't open until six. Four A.M. alarm for me, so I'm a little ahead of the game." Ted's voice boomed in the quiet bakery.

"Hey Dad, I've got some good news! Despite the really cold weather, everything is okay in the building so far. No power outages, and the pipes are running smoothly." Joy says.

"That's great to hear. I wanted to walk through the front doors, but I noticed the snow levels at the backdoor, so I decided to come in that way after shoveling. I wanted to make the front page of *The Newberry News* the first-ever customer in The Northern Bites' history. Yoopers like me get a kick out of small things like that. That headline sure would beat the weekly drug bust and deaths taking over the main page every week."

"How about we give you the honor of flipping the open sign, Ted?" Willis asks.

"It would be my honor. I've never had an open sign in my sawmill," Ted replies, flipping the Northern Bites sign over to open.

Within minutes of flipping the open sign, to Willis and Joy's surprise, even with the record-breaking cold temperatures, a line starts to form quickly, running out the front door. The line continued till the end of the business day, as the whole town came out.

"What a day," Willis says, sitting down behind the register, soaking in the day after closing.

"For not knowing what we were doing, I thought we did pretty well today. I hope we can find some reliable help soon. We are about out of everything, so I need you to run to the IGA before they close so I can get started baking for tomorrow. I'll make you up a list, and don't forget a 'we're hiring' flier to put up," Joy says.

Willis makes his way to the grocery store, looking for items on Joy's supply list. Several locals greet Willis on opening day, while others avoid him, not trusting that the outsider has the best interests of the town or the Newberry Building at heart. Putting up his now-hiring flier on the bulletin board on his way out, A missing person poster was right next to where Willis found an opening to place his flier. The faded photograph showed a young woman with sun-kissed hair and a smile that mirrored Joy's in a way that sent a jolt through him. Her name, Tiffany, did little to dispel the unsettling resemblance. The unease gnawed at him. Was this just a coincidence, a trick of memory, or a chilling premonition? The once-simple question of picking up groceries now felt laced with a new, terrifying possibility: could this ever happen to Joy?

CHAPTER 11

As the frigid winter months dragged on relentlessly, Northern Bites continued to flourish and gain momentum. Despite the harsh weather conditions, the restaurant managed to entice many new patrons. The warm and inviting environment was a welcome respite from the biting cold outside. Over time, these new customers became regulars.

First to gain the title of regular's status at Northern Bites are Bob and Mike. Both Mike and Bob have never missed a day since the bakery opened its doors. They arrive every morning at Northern Bites at the same time just before the morning rush, and they spend time watching people and telling their stories of old days in Newberry. When Bob looks at you, you can see on his face that the years have been tough on him, and he has many stories to tell. Bob is a short gray-haired man with a raspy voice, which adds to his strong persona and makes him even more memorable. He has dedicated his life to serving his community and used to be the police chief of Newberry. Unfortunately, due to funding cuts, the police force was disbanded, leaving Bob without a job, so he decided to retire. Bob is never seen without his hat on, and he walks with a limp from a gunshot wound. He quickly clarifies that the injury was from a hunting trip and not from the line of duty.

Then there's Mike, who looks a decade older than Bob with a scratchy smoker's voice, thick-rimmed glasses and a handlebar mustache, who became the first customer to create their own drink on the menu called 'The 911', which is four shots of espresso with dark roast coffee. Bob carries most of the morning conversation, sharing bits and pieces of past local stories and bragging about his dog, Malko, who hangs out in his truck while he visits Northern Bites. Mike usually shares the latest wild rumors and off-color jokes that would make a comedian blush, along with other wild tales of his past years of wild nightlife around Newberry over the decades.

Among the new customers, another name that stands out from the others with no lack of character at Northern Bites is Larry Burke. He stands out among the locals in Newberry because he wears suits and ties, as if he is going to work in a skyscraper in downtown Chicago or Detroit rather than in the middle of the Upper Peninsula wilderness. Larry is not afraid to speak his mind, and he has a strong passion for pointing out what he sees as the problems in the village. He also doesn't trust the local government officials, who he believes conduct shady dealings behind closed doors. Larry has a vast collection of colorful scarves, and he seems to wear a different one every day. It's possible that his collection is a memento of his travels around the world. If possible, Larry buys a scarf for every destination, so each scarf comes with a long story behind it. In the past, Larry served on many community committees but resigned before being kicked out by most of them. During a village council meeting, Larry revealed he had a run-in with some village elites and the village manager over embezzling funds, which caused so much heat that he was escorted out. The fact that Larry was not on any local boards or committees didn't slow him down. Stepping away from local politics allowed him to have a louder voice. Larry started a local opinion newspaper called Freedom for Newberry. He is known for attending every council meeting and delivering lengthy, passionate speeches. Due to his speeches, the board changed the limits for public comments. Larry is also known for creating pre-recorded videos filled with wild conspiracies that have become a local favorite. These videos are usually aired immediately after Newberry Village meetings.

While cleaning up the restrooms after a busy morning, Willis hears the door chime and rushes out to assist. He finds Larry Burke standing at the counter, leaning over, and trying to see if there is anyone in the back.

"I thought this town might have scared you off. I was going to help myself to some tea and muffins," Larry says jokingly to Willis.

"Just cleaning up while I get a brief break," Willis responds.

"I like the various vintage photo additions you keep adding to this bakery. The local history you showcase, like the logging photos, truly captures what this area is about. It looks like you've done a little research on the area. Didn't you work on a newspaper before moving here?" Larry asks, looking around the room at the artwork.

"I used to work as an entertainment reporter for the *Kansas City Star* and always aspired to be part of the investigative reporting team. However, they rejected me, stating that I needed more experience. My dad started a local newspaper when I was six. He called the paper *The Pony Express* after the Pony Express riders that had their start in Missouri. My family lived and breathed the news. I can remember my dad Murray always telling people the newspaper would never be like the other local paper's that avoided the hard-hitting stories instead for the fluff pieces just to sell papers. I hated the newspaper most of my childhood; there's a real emptiness without my dad's columns to read. He had such a way with words."

"How long ago did your father pass away?" Larry asks.

"He passed eight years ago; we hardly had a chance to say goodbye as the stage four cancer moved quickly. My mom and I had to figure out what to do with the paper after he passed away. I had already moved away from Joplin to Kansas City and had a great career. My father told my mother not to let me move back to run it, as I had my own story to tell. The paper was my father, and no one could ever replace him. My mother ended up selling the newspaper to a large regional newspaper publisher. The paper isn't the same, but it lives on, at least. Journalism is in my blood," Willis shares.

"You said it's in your blood, so who knows, you might be surprised, especially in a little town with loads of dark secrets still hidden in these woods. I know my paper may seem radical, but if you're ever interested, I could put your investigative skills to work for my independent paper, Freedom for Newberry." Larry says.

"You never know; maybe someday. Speaking of secrets, I've noticed numerous missing person posters around town, but no one is talking about it."

"This town's got a tight-lipped reputation. Prying won't get you far, but a shared drink with a local might loosen things up and unleash a treasure trove of untold stories! Being a town that lives or dies off of tourism, these stories are usually kept out of the media. Sadly, those missing person posters don't usually last when hung up. Not many locals are aware of the truth. Those secrets never leave the woods. Some around here want the least amount of change and try to control what does change. Over the years, I've seen a handful of great places and ideas start just to be run out of town. I'm not saying it's impossible to do something here, but you don't want to get on the wrong side of certain people or families in the area," Larry warns Willis.

"Certain people?" Willis asks as he cleans his espresso machine.

"It won't be long till you find out who I'm talking about. If you want to know, just chat with some old-timers with deep roots in Newberry, like Bob and Mike; they know who I'm talking about. Your father-in-law should have some stories for sure; just mention the family names Porters and Hughes," Larry says.

"Ted's memory is a bottomless well of tales that man's a human library! Ted and I take the old Finnish road every time we ride together. I hear the same stories on every bumpy, slow ride on that dirt road. Newberry sure has stories for being just over one hundred and fifty years old," Willis says.

"The stories you hear are only the beginning; the real interesting and messed-up stuff you have to dig deep to find out. Newberry may be a young village, but the stories run deep. What happened in those logging camps in Dollarville shaped not only Newberry but the whole Upper Peninsula. Sadly, some people paid the highest price, and that's the Native Americans around this area. You should ask Ted about the old Native American town that burned down years ago in Newberry. You probably drive by that area every day and didn't realize a whole native tribe lived here for generations before the logging community drove them out of their homes," Larry says.

"Hold on a second, Burke. There are always rumors swirling around this village, but have you seen any real evidence about the Porters and the Hughes? Without those families, this area would still be wilderness. The truth is, the natives set the fire themselves and made out like bandits with the land they got south of town," Mike says, rebuking Larry.

"That's what sells newspapers, Mike, but it's not what happened. You can't just burn the past away, though some around here think you can. To find the truth in this town, you have to search for yourself. You have to dig until you find what really happened, but sometimes you'll find out things you wish you hadn't."

"It sounds like this village might have some deep secrets," Willis says.

"You don't know the half of it. There's no way the recent mobile home explosion in town was an accident," Larry responds.

As Mike and Larry debate back and forth about the history of the village until Larry leaves in frustration, storming out, Willis hears the creaking of the back entrance swing open. Willis remembers it's noon, and his first new hire for Northern Bites is starting today, Chelsea.

"So sorry I'm late," Chelsea says, taking off her gray beanie, revealing her long black hair with purple highlights underneath, then putting her shivering hands together to warm them after taking off her gloves. "I had to drop my daughter off at my best friend Sarah's house. The county plow hadn't made it to her road, so I had to walk the rest of the way in to drop my daughter off."

"That's no problem; glad you made it," Willis says, helping Chelsea find a place to put her things.

"I didn't know if I should come in the backdoor or the front. I knew I was running late, so I tried the back first," Chelsea responds, still shivering and adjusting to the warmth in the room from the outside chill.

"I live upstairs and hardly leave this building, so I can cover if you ever run late. I know raising kids can be tricky; I have a son. You'll get to know my son, Archer, soon enough. He likes to peek around the corners to see what's happening in the bakery, so don't think you see a ghost running around the doorways; it's just my son."

"Are you going to introduce us or not?" Mike asked, leaning back in his seat, waiting for a response.

"Mike and Bob, this is Chelsea, the newest member of the Northern Bites family," Willis says, motioning to Chelsea as she waves with a smile to Bob and Mike.

"The only team member, you mean? Everyone else is too scared to work for you," Bob says while taking a sip of his coffee and looking at Mike with a grin.

"Thank you for saving us from Willis's stories. If he took longer to hire some help, an ambulance would be pulling him out of here on a stretcher," Mike says.

"Mike, you watch it, or I'll slip you decaf in that triple espresso," Willis says jokingly.

"You wouldn't dare," Mike says with a fake shocked look and his hands in the air in response.

"I could never do that, and you know it, Mike. I would hate to see what you are like without caffeine running through your veins," Willis replies sarcastically.

"It's a nightmare for everyone around." Mike says.

"Taking note, never decaf for either Bob or Mike, or the world might end," Chelsea replies.

"This girl has already won me over. Seeing Chelsea will surely beat looking at your ugly mug first thing in the morning," Bob says sarcastically to Willis.

"Sorry, boys, but she's going to help in the afternoons, so this ugly mug is all you'll see in the mornings," Willis says, causing both Bob and Mike each to lay out a loud sigh.

"Well, welcome to the team, Chelsea; you'll do great, and if you don't, you bet we will blame it on Willis anyway," Mike says, getting up from his chair.

"I guess I will let Willis train you in peace, but if he makes it hard on you, let us know, and we will take care of him," Bob says, giving Chelsea a wink.

CHAPTER 12

The next day, on a sunny yet frosty morning, another one of Willis's regulars, Neal, comes into Northern Bites to start the business day. The unique thing that took Willis a few visits to figure out was what Neal did for a living, as he always came in with a different hair color or facial hair style every couple of visits. After a few weeks, Neal shared that he works as an undercover narcotics agent across the Upper Peninsula. From a heavy beard to a handlebar mustache, Willis has already seen multiple versions of Neal. Neal's natural red hair is difficult to hide with the growth, but if you didn't know him, you'd think he had a personality disorder. Neal rarely discusses cases involving the Newberry area but enjoys getting Willis's take on what's happening around town. He's usually sent on cases to the west side of the Upper Peninsula or to Sault Ste. Marie to protect his family. It's been a few days since Neal last visited Northern Bites, so Willis is looking forward to hearing what's happening around the Upper Peninsula, or at least as much as Neal can usually share, which is more than Willis expects to hear usually.

"Mornin," Neal says in his deep voice, sporting a long black beard this time with a black Carhartt hat, a red flannel shirt, and black-rimmed glasses.

"That beard grew fast; if I didn't know you so well now, I wouldn't have recognized you, Neal," Willis says.

"This is a fake, and it itches," Neal says, grabbing onto his beard, revealing red growth underneath.

"On the news last night, the reporter talked about a drug raid in Sault Ste. Marie. Did you help with that one?" Willis asks.

"Sadly, I did. Some of my old college roommates from Superior State were arrested in the raid. I hate when someone you know is involved in a bust. That's why I like to travel as far away as possible, but it seems like the hot spot right now is more in the eastern Upper Peninsula. The whole raid went quickly and safely. My unit was after a group of higher-level dealers, but the people we wanted to catch never showed up. Someone must've tipped them off, and now we might have to start all over again to catch them unless one of those arrested decides to rat them out if they even knew the dealers. Is there anything new drug-related around here in Newberry?" Neal asks.

"Two days ago, a correctional officer's house exploded just outside town. Luckily, no one was inside at the time. The state police found drugs around the officer's home, and he caused quite a scene when they arrested him on the job at the prison, some of the locals told me yesterday," Willis shares.

"I'm surprised I never heard about this, but I've been overwhelmed with getting ready for the bust in the Soo. Never a dull week in Newberry. Glad to hear no one was hurt. I'll have to check into that explosion," Neal responds.

"Another thing that I can't get off my mind is the number of missing people in the area over the last couple of years I've either heard or read about since moving here. Two months ago, I saw a missing person flyer of a girl who resembled my wife, Joy. I believe her name was Tiffany. I took a picture of the poster on my phone. Let me pull it up for you," Willis says, grabbing his phone, scrolling through his pictures, and then showing Neal. "She doesn't look like anyone I've seen around town. So much has changed in Newberry in a short time. Growing up in

Newberry, this village was always known as a safe and peaceful area, a true step back in time to better days. People never thought about locking their homes. You could even leave your truck running while doing a grocery run. Sadly, those days are over thanks to the high level of drug use around town. Meth, heroin, and fentanyl are all over these streets, causing people to do some terrible things to themselves and others. You would be surprised at how many nice homes the narcotics team raids around here compared to those that look like drug houses. Some of the best people I've met got hooked on these rough drugs, and it's a quick downhill spiral. We arrested a mailman a few weeks ago for distributing heroin near the high school to teenagers At first, all the hard drugs came to the area from Milwaukee and Detroit through a local drug ring, but now we don't know how they're getting here. The harder we push, the harder it seems they are pushing back. All the leads seem to run into a brick wall. The fear is so deep that people would rather go to prison than say who is behind the drug ring around here. Someone is putting fear into the locals. Have you ever heard the name Mother Mary mentioned around the bakery by chance?" Neal asks.

"Only in church," Willis responds.

"Not that, Mary, the complete opposite. This Mary is the devil in human form. She got the nickname from being the drug lord up here in the Upper Peninsula that all started right here in downtown Newberry," Neal replies.

"No, this is the first time," Willis says.

"Good. Mary started the uptick in crime and drugs in this area in the late 1990s. I helped put her behind bars five years ago. But word is, she found a way out recently and is coming back to town," Neal says.

As the morning moves along without much business traffic in Northern Bites, Neal shares with Willis more about Mother Mary. Neal explains the way the village was once a perfect example of the American dream, where you could let your children walk around the town unsupervised. Newberry was a great small town to raise a family in until Mary got hooked on drugs, then it all unraveled. Mary began with low-level illegal things like weed and bootleg liquor. Over time, Mary's deals started getting worse as she started to bring meth and heroin into the area. At first, you never would have guessed Mary was the one behind the drugs moving into Newberry. Around town, Mary was known as the lady other women wanted to be. Her family, for generations, ran the only ladies clothing store in town. As she got more hooked on harder drugs, you could see the change in Mary's appearance. After costing countless people's lives and their loved ones so much pain, she was caught and put in prison. Even after going to prison twice, Mary always ended up back in Newberry, causing trouble again. That was until five years ago. Neal shares how he worked with the Upper Peninsula substance enforcement team called Upset, a multi-jurisdictional narcotics task force that serves all across the Upper Peninsula of Michigan, to finally put a stop to Mary, now in her late sixties, taking her down on multiple charges. She was taken out of the Upper Peninsula to the prison in Jackson, Michigan. Neal brings up that recently, Mary reached a plea deal the FBI couldn't pass on, and now she is free. Neal suggests that the drug rings probably paid for Mary's lawyers to protect her. Neal shares that his brother, Rick, started using opioids because of Mary, and he died from overdosing eight years ago so stopping Mary and the current drug ring is very personal to him in many ways. Willis asks what she looks like now, and Neal describes that if Willis sees an old gray-haired lady walking around with a cane and wearing an eye patch over her right eye, that's Mother Mary. Neal warns Willis that

57

even a Mary older is still incredibly dangerous. Mother Mary could go anywhere, but if she returns to Newberry, it's for only one thing, and that's revenge. Neal hands Willis a business card and asks him to call if he ever hears or sees to get in touch with him right away.

CHAPTER 13

Two months later

After school, a boy runs into Northern Bites, beating the usual after-school rush.

"Could I put up a flyer?" the boy asks Willis, looking up at him from the other side of the counter, looking worried about something.

Willis wonders if bullies are chasing the boy. So he briefly takes a look out the front windows, seeing that the boy is alone and not being followed. He looked over at the posters by the entrance door, which is currently filled, and noticed some old events that needed to come down that happened earlier in the week.

"Do you see that one on the right that says raffle on it?" Willis asks, pointing at the raffle flyer with the boy turning around.

"Yes," the boy replies.

"That would be a great spot. You can take that down the flyer and put yours right in its place," Willis tells the boy.

"Thank you. Can I get a strawberry smoothie?" the boy adds, smiling and digging in his pocket for money, coming up short of the amount needed for the drink.

"How about today? This one's on the house for bringing me in a brand-new flyer and for being a loyal customer," Willis says, smiling at the boy.

"I'll be back tomorrow with another flyer then," the boy responds, his face lighting up in excitement.

"Don't spread the news with the other kids, or I will end up broke. This is a secret one-day deal just for you," Willis says, handing the boy his drink.

"It's our secret, I promise," the boy replies, walking towards the exit, setting down his drink on a table to put up his flyer, then waving bye to Willis as he walks out, sipping on his drink.

After cleaning up, Willis comes from behind the counter, curious to see what was on the flyer. Any event this time of year is something to celebrate, as things slow down with the most challenging part of winter settling in. As Willis looks at the flyer, he notices it was not just another fish fry or fundraiser flyer, but a new missing person poster. This time is different, though. Willis knows the face and name on the poster, Sarah. The hairs on his arm raise in shock as he soaks in that Noah's fiancée, Sarah, is the one missing. Sarah's also a close friend of Chelsea's. Sarah and Chelsea are like sisters from the stories Chelsea's shared over the months, even bringing in Ava, Sarah's daughter, for a treat every once in a while when off work.

Willis quickly texts Joy.

"You need to come down when you can," Willis types.

"Did you break something?" Joy texts back from upstairs at their home.

"No, a boy just brought in a missing person flyer, and it's Noah's fiancée, Sarah," Willis types back.

Before Willis can send Joy an image of the flyer, she comes downstairs and stands next to him.

"That was quick; I was just about to send you a picture of the flyer to see if you could help me get the word out. I

60

need to somehow reach out to Noah to see if there's anything I can do to help."

"Oh no, not little Sarah," Joy responded, covering her mouth in fear, with tears rolling down her cheeks. "I never saw Sarah when she came on opening day with Noah like you did. I never expected Sarah, the little girl I used to babysit when she was only five or six years old while I was in high school, to be Noah's fiancée. When I watched Sarah, she could get away with anything. Her beautiful smile, big blue eyes, and long black hair were too adorable." Joy shares. "She will be okay; someone will find her soon," Willis says, putting his arms around Joy.

"Oh no, Chelsea! She's supposed to be coming in for the last couple of hours of work coverage for me. I wonder if she has any idea yet. I should call her and have her take time off," Willis says.

"I wouldn't call her. Chelsea must have been one of the first to discover or report her disappearance. Doesn't Sarah watch Chelsea's daughter, and aren't they best friends?" Joy asks.

"You're right, if Chelsea doesn't make it in for her shift, I will probably close down Northern Bites early. No one is going to be running around town with Sarah missing. Right now, it's not safe to go outside, so please don't take Archer out unless I am with you or you're with your parents. What's happening around here?" Willis asked.

"I've been away from Newberry for ten years, and everything looks the same, but something's changed that you can't see."

"Maybe I should call Chelsea just to let her know we care and not to come in. She needs to be out there looking for Sarah. Not working on a day like this."

Willis steps over towards the event room, where he gets the most reliable cell signal in the building. He tries to reach Chelsea, but the call is sent straight to voicemail. Willis decides not to leave a message and tries to call again, but the call goes straight to voicemail for the second time. Without knowing the words to say, Willis just hangs up.

"I'll stay here with you," Joy responds to Willis, seeing him not reach Chelsea by phone.

"Sounds like the right move. The last thing I want to do is say the wrong thing in a time like this," Willis says to Joy as a couple of customers enter Northern Bites. Greeting them with a hello, Willis walks behind the counter to take their order, while Joy continues to examine the missing person flyer, writing down the number at the bottom.

While Willis tries to gather his thoughts as he makes the customer's order, he hears the back door open. Moments later, Chelsea walks around the corner Willis greets Chelsea with a smile, but he notices that her smile back seems forced. It's not like her usual chipper greeting. Chelsea silently walks to the prep area to wash her hands and put on her apron.

Willis glanced at Joy after handing the to-go order to the customers who were now leaving Northern Bites. He signaled to Joy, not knowing what to do next with Chelsea. Joy walked over to him behind the counter to assist with the situation.

"Is everything okay?" Joy asked Chelsea softly as she put on her apron in the prep area. Chelsea didn't respond to Joy's question until they made eye contact. As soon as they locked eyes, Chelsea burst into tears and fell to her knees, crying on the floor in the back prep area. Joy kneeled beside her to console her.

"Everything will be all right, Chelsea. We are so sorry; we just heard about Sarah a few minutes ago. We're here to help. There will be endless searches for her, and we will get her back home as soon as possible," Joy says, hugging Chelsea.

"No one has ever returned who goes missing here, nobody," Chelsea says, crying on Joy's shoulder.

"This time will be different," Willis says, looking over at Joy and Chelsea, with Chelsea still crying on Joy's shoulder.

Joy looks over at Willis, giving him a 'no' nod and a shush gesture with her finger for him to keep quiet as she "comforts Chelsea.

"We can go look for Sarah with you; does that sound good?" Joy asks Chelsea, sniffing and trying to pull herself back together.

"You don't have to do that," Chelsea says as she starts to stand up with Joy's help.

"I'm going to lock up Northern Bites for the day and then check if Archer is up from his afternoon nap. Chelsea, we will do everything in our power to help you locate Sarah. I'll be back down with Archer right away," Willis says, locking the front door and then heading up the stairs to get his son.

"Do you want us to watch your daughter Bethany for you? Archer will love having her around," Joy asks Chelsea as they wait for Willis and Archer to come down.

"I have no idea what I'm going to do right now. All I want is to find Sarah and get her back home to Ava. Yesterday, I saw Sarah for a short time. I could tell something was off about her. She tries to just hold it in, but I can read her like a book. I tried to get what was bothering her out of her, but she wouldn't tell me a thing and changed the subject. She said it was just a headache, but I know her and could tell it was more than that. I thought it might be about Noah, but we ended up discussing a silly reality TV show we were both watching. I should've pressed her more. I just knew something was bothering her. My gut feeling is that I think she knew what was going to happen. Sarah's the last person I would ever think we would see on one of those missing person posters," Chelsea says, crying again.

"That just made me think of something. I wonder if there's somehow a connection between all these local people going missing," Joy says, walking over to her iPad with Chelsea following.

"I hope not, but that's a good idea, Joy. No one has ever returned from any of the missing people posters I've seen in town; they just vanish," Chelsea says, looking over Joy's shoulder as she starts searching.

Joy types in the search bar "Newberry missing people," and her search brings up five stories covering different missing people over the last two years in Newberry.

"Do you know any of these names or recognize any of their faces, Chelsea?" Joy asks, pointing at the images on the iPad.

"Some of these faces look familiar from seeing them around town, but I don't know any of them. Most of my friends and family are in my close circle." Chelsea says. As she examines the pictures, she pays close attention to every detail.

"Maybe we should show these images to Willis. Willis always dreamed of becoming an investigative reporter because he loved uncovering the truth. One of the things that made me fall in love with Willis is how he won't stop looking until he finds the answers. He never gives up," Joy tells Chelsea.

"Hmm, this is strange. Joe Benjamin made all these posters. Look, his name is at the bottom of every one of these posts online, along with his contact details if anyone has any information about the missing person's whereabouts." Chelsea replied, pointing at the screen.

"You know him?" Joy asks.

"I know Joe well, or at least I used to. Joe was like a brother to Sarah and me when we were little. He is one of the Ojibway kids, like Sarah and me. Joe lives next door to my mom's house on the reservation. We used to be super close, but he's become a shut-in more and more since his serious car accident that paralyzed him from the waist down. I remember Joe had all sorts of hockey scholarships, but when a semi-truck hit him after a prospect tournament in Traverse City on his way back home, everything changed for him. Now when I see Joe, it's just a wave from his wheelchair as I walk into my mom's house."

"I think you should try to talk to Joe," Joy suggests.

"I'll get in touch with him soon. We Ojibway, we always watch out for each other."

In full snow gear, Willis walks down the stairs with Archer in his arms all bundled up.

"Okay, let's find Sarah," Willis says.

"Where are we going, Willis?" Joy asks.

"Anywhere and everywhere. Maybe something is being put together for a search at the school."

"You might want to drive to the school. Those winds outside right now cut like a knife," Chelsea says.

"Chelsea, would you like to come with us?" Willis asks.

"Sure, you both are too kind to me; I don't deserve it Most people would likely judge me as emotionally unstable and have fired me. You both being here right now means so much to me."

Willis, Joy, Archer, and Chelsea load into Willis's SUV and drive up a few blocks to the school. When they arrive at the school, people are walking in from all directions, and the parking lot is nearly impossible to find a parking space in. After finding a parking spot, Willis and the others follow the crowd as they head into the school towards the main auditorium. Inside the auditorium, every seat is filled, making it standing room only. Willis leans against the auditorium's back wall with his family as Chelsea is asked to sit with Sarah's daughter Ava and her family. Noah is next to them on the front row, looking like his soul has been ripped from his body, with Sarah vanishing. The newly promoted principal of Tahquamenon Area School, Susan Porter, takes to the podium to thank everyone who came out on such short notice. The public's rapid response shows the community's heart for Sarah and the tight-knit nature of Newberry's residents.

As the meeting progresses, the Newberry Fire Department and Michigan State Police divide the attendees into search parties. This is to ensure that as much ground is covered as quickly as possible. Each group is handed a local map with areas in and around the county to search for Sarah. The principal of the high school uses a projector to display the last known location of Sarah and what she was wearing when last seen. The principal concluded the search by inviting a local pastor to lead the attendees in prayer for Sarah's safe return.

A man next to Willis leans over, talking quietly to Willis as the search meeting for Sarah closes.

"I hate that the only times you see everyone get along in this town is at funerals or a tragedy. No matter the personal issues, all that stops when things happen to one of our own," the man says to Willis.

"How did you hear about this?" Willis asks.

"I found out minutes ago driving through town, listening to the radio. I noticed a large crowd outside the school, so I just pulled over and came in. I guess as soon as the posters of Sarah started popping up all over town, everyone had the same idea to do something about it."

The news spread around the village of Newberry like wildfire, with hundreds of flashlights roaming everywhere you turned. The tribal police on the reservation and other tribal groups from around the Upper Peninsula look for any signs of foul play or evidence left behind by her. Search groups ventured deep into the snow-filled woods, walking miles down next to the railroad tracks, snowmobiles riding down the trails, and even some went out kayaking in the half-frozen swamps and rivers looking for any sign of Sarah. No stone was left unturned in and around Newberry. Every door, garage, and alleyway in the village was checked with no trace of the beloved hometown girl, Sarah.

On the second day of the search, while deep in the woods riding through trails in a pine plantation, a snowmobiler finds a colorful, bright pink sneaker not covered by the snow. The Michigan State Police brought Sarah's family into the police offices to see if the shoe could've been Sarah's, and they recognized it as one of her favorite pairs. The search teams focused on that area for days, but nothing else appeared to connect with Sarah.

The news of a missing Native American girl from Newberry ignited fear and concern across Northern Michigan. Search parties joined in from across the Upper Peninsula, from below the Mackinac Bridge, all the way to Grand Rapids, Michigan. The DNR and fishermen kept checking down the Tahquamenon and Two Hearted Rivers to the rock-covered shores of Lake Superior. In just a few days, search parties covered every inch of the search area multiple times. Despite their efforts, only a few potential leads were found, which unfortunately turned out to be dead ends other than the pink sneaker. As a result, the small village of Newberry, Sarah's friends, and her family were left with little hope. As time passes since the last appearance of Sarah, the community loses hope of finding her. Rumors began to spread that Sarah didn't want to be found and ran away.

Sarah's absence cast a long shadow over Newberry. The detectives spread out to conduct interviews and piece together the events leading up to her disappearance. Noah found himself at the center of the community's attention and under intense scrutiny from the detectives, as he was the last person known to have seen her alive.

As Willis and Joy would drive back and forth between their home and her parents, Willis would look over at Noah's house, which was on the way between the two. Some days Willis would see multiple Michigan State Police cars at Noah's home searching all over the property, which could be quite the task, as Noah was known as the collector of anything anyone else didn't want in the area, his home being one step away from a junk yard. Noah had a habit of never giving away anything he could find a use for someday, which was common in an area like Newberry with limited shopping options, but Noah took it to the extreme. Willis couldn't help but wonder what all this interrogating was doing to Noah, being alone and wanting to be out searching with everyone for Sarah.

"I can't imagine what Noah is suffering through right now. It's just unbelievable that she's still missing, and Noah can't do a thing to help with the State Police Department and FBI viewing him still as a possible suspect," Willis says.

"I hate to ask, but do you think Noah had anything to do with it?" Joy asks.

"Never. I can't picture Noah doing something like that."

"Maybe Sarah had enough and tried to leave Noah, and he lost it, and she ran away," Joy responds.

"How could Sarah just leave behind her daughter, her car, everything? It doesn't make sense, and she would've told someone close what's happening," Willis responds frustratedly.

Joy's voice trembled with a raw conviction. "Sarah's absence hangs heavy in this town. Someone here knows what happened, and that truth will find a way out. We can't just pretend everything's normal."

Willis, his face etched with empathy, nodded solemnly. "You're right, Joy. This whole community is hurting. Especially those close to her. How can you move on when a piece of you is missing? Sarah deserves answers, and we owe it to her to never stop looking. Consider me all in."

"This isn't a television show, Willis. This situation is real. The whole mess makes me scared to go outside. I never thought I would feel that way in Newberry, but I do now. I used to walk down these streets with my friends, never thinking of anything terrible happening to us. Maybe I was just naive, but Newberry felt that way. I love this village so much that I hope things turn around."

"I do too," Willis replies in a somber voice.

That night, back at Willis's home on the second floor in The Newberry Building, right before bed, Willis decided to turn on the local news out of Marquette. Willis checks the local news to see if anyone has any information about the ongoing search for Sarah. As local nightly news anchors are giving updates on the latest road issues and wild weather heading in over the weekend, the anchor cuts to breaking news of an active shooting in Gould City, a small town close to Newberry. Gould City usually never makes the news, and Willis realizes this must be significantly bigger than usual. The Gould City shooting forces Willis to sit up and move to the end of the bed, intently watching as Joy tries to go to sleep next to him.

"Hope you're turning that off soon; it's so bright. Can you turn it off?" Joy asks with a grunt of frustration, trying to block the light from the television with pillows between her and Willis.

"A shooting happened in Gould City and made breaking news. I'll go watch in the living room and keep it down."

"They always say it's breaking news. I'm stealing one of your pillows," Joy says as she grabs one of Willis's pillows and covers her head.

Willis turns off the television in his bedroom and quietly walks down the hallway to his living room. As he enters the living room, Willis pulls up a chair close to the television and turns it on, keeping the volume down and turning his attention back to the breaking news story out of Gould City.

"We return to our breaking news at The Dirty Elk Hotel in Gould City, where multiple people have been shot tonight within the last hour. Our reporter, Janice, is now in Gould City with the latest. Janice, can you tell us what's currently happening?" the news anchor asks the reporter at the Dirty Elk Hotel, with police and ambulance lights flashing behind her.

"I'm standing in front of the Dirty Elk Hotel, and the state police are investigating a shooting involving multiple people. At this time, the shooter is unknown and still at large," the reporter says, while a body on a stretcher is rolled behind her into an ambulance by two EMTs.

"Do we know anything about what caused this incident?" The anchor asks the reporter.

"The Michigan State Police have informed us that multiple shots were fired with numerous injuries at the scene over the last hour at this time. The Dirty Elk Hotel is now an active crime scene, and locals should take an alternate route. US-2 is currently blocked, and a temporary detour is in place. The reasoning behind the multiple shootings is unclear at this time. Numerous eyewitnesses saw a man leave in a red pickup truck, and the state police are currently in pursuit. Please contact your local police or the sheriff's department for any information about seeing a red pickup truck. The sheriff's department requests that, at this time, everyone who does not need to travel in the area should please lock their homes and stay inside. If you notice any unusual activity near you, please do not try to take matters into your own hands. This man is said to be armed and extremely dangerous.

"Thank you, Janice. Just in from Saint Ignace, a toll booth operator disappears without a trace while on duty at the Mackinac Bridge toll booths. We are following this developing story and will bring you more details as they become available. Residents are advised to stay home at this time for their safety. If you have any information, please call the state police. Tomorrow morning, we will have a live update from Gould City on the active fugitive and those involved in the shooting, and from Saint Ignace. Stay safe, everyone," the news anchor says from the news desk before the station returns to its regular programming.

"Stay safe? Yeah, right. Between the fugitive on the loose, Sarah's disappearance, and now a missing toll booth attendant, a good night's sleep seemed like a distant memory," Willis muttered to himself, the words barely a whisper.

Willis turned off the television, the blaring news replaced by an unnerving quiet. He slowly walked down the hall, his steps heavy with worry. Outside Archer's room, he paused, stealing a glimpse of his son. Tucked under the covers, bathed in the soft glow of a nightlight, Archer slept peacefully, oblivious to the growing darkness that swirled around the village.

"What did I get us into?" Willis says to himself, shaking his head and thinking about the world he's put himself and his family into.

Willis enters his room, moving slowly into bed, trying not to wake Joy.

"Was it breaking news?" Joy asks, half asleep next to Willis, a few seconds after he laid down next to her.

"It's nothing that can't wait until morning," Willis says, keeping the bad news about the killings and fugitive on the run for in the morning, knowing Joy would be up for hours.

CHAPTER 14

The following day, after a rough night's sleep, Willis opens Northern Bites as usual. Willis pulled a few extra espresso shots to fill his morning kick-off cup of coffee to help with the lack of sleep. The first customers of this rainy Saturday morning are Bob and Mike, who come in at their usual time, like clockwork.

"Did you catch the news on The Dirty Elk and that missing lady working the toll booth at the Mackinac Bridge?" Mike asks.

"Sadly, I saw the story on the news right as I tried to go to sleep. I didn't sleep well knowing someone's running from the law in the area. Who knows, maybe that person is still armed and desperate, looking for a place that's open to making more problems. My mind couldn't calm down last night," Willis replies, then yawns.

"Yeah, Willis, you look rougher than usual, like a semi hit you, and the day's just beginning," Bob says, looking at Willis as he sits at his favorite table.

"I hope this extra espresso I just had fixes that," Willis says, pouring Bob and Mike's daily coffees.

"I caught the Dirty Elk story this morning on the news. Things go wrong around there all the time, it seems. That's just terrible to hear, and you can bet that some people from Newberry are bound to be involved in it. The Dirty Elk should've shut down long ago, and it's ridiculous that a place like that can stay open. I hope this is the final nail in its coffin. You would think an act of God would have turned that dump into ash. Last year, my son was shot twice when he was part of the undercover unit during a drug bust at that hotel," Mike says angrily.

"I didn't even know you had a son. I thought I knew everything about you by now," Willis said, bringing over Mike and Bob's drinks.

"He's your age, early thirties. My son's name is Shane. I'm proud of that boy; he's one of the good ones trying to keep this area safe and moving in a better direction. Shane was part of the Upper Peninsula Upset uncover unit for seven years and loved every minute of it until he took two bullets at the Dirty Elk. One of the bullets damaged his right arm badly, and the other hit close to his left eye, forever affecting his eyesight. Now he works as a correctional officer at the prison in the business offices, doing paperwork. My son hates it and misses being in the field. Bob here trained my son as a deputy," Mike says, pointing over at Bob.

"Your son is still one of the finest, Mike. I'm not just saying that since you bought the coffee this morning," Bob says with a half-laugh.

"I buy it every morning. Isn't that right, Willis?" Mike asked.

"You're not wrong, Mike," Willis replies.

"I don't know how such a great young man came from you, but you did something right," Bob says jokingly to Mike.

"The shootings kept me up for a while, working through who was involved and why. When my mind gets started, I don't have an off switch till I find an answer. Did they mention anything new about The Dirty Elk or any update on the shooter this morning?"

"The state police shared it was a man who shot three people, killing one and seriously injuring the other two. The police tracked down the shooter's truck left at a boat launch by Big Manistique Lake over in Curtis, but there was no trace of him other than some tire tracks. It looks like he arranged for someone to pick him up. The police are checking all the houses around that area this morning to see who saw or heard anything. Sadly, most people in those homes are snowbirds this time of the year, enjoying the sun in Arizona or some other hot weather place that those thin skins hideout at till spring arrives. Finding someone who saw or heard anything late at night will be hard. The highest chance of getting any evidence will be from those back at The Dirty Elk. Someone at the hotel will know something, unless it was just a random act. Sometimes, people just get crazy and do stupid stuff. From what I'm hearing, whoever did that last night left a mess," Bob shares.

"From what you just told me and the news last night, we still have someone who doesn't mind killing on the loose, possibly even closer to town. Now we have a killer and two missing people in our community, gone without a trace. I hope to God that Sarah wasn't one of those injured at The Dirty Elk last night," Willis says.

"I don't think Sarah was there last night. We would've heard something by now, Willis. They didn't mention her this morning," Bob shares.

"So, what's next with Sarah?" Willis asks Bob.

"Well, first off, the state units are looking for three missing people, and one's crazy armed and dangerous, and that's getting all the attention right now. Anything connected to finding Sarah will be at the local level, and we are the local level ourselves. The families of those missing people will never give up hope, but this town has a history of becoming weary and moving on quickly from these situations. People push their feelings aside for those they've lost, trying to hide the hurt. What you are doing right now is the best thing you can do to help find Sarah, and that's keeping talking about her. Since I retired from the local police, opioids have taken over for meth around here, and it's an addictive mess. The hospital here in town deals with people overdosing now more than anything else, but you'll never hear a word about it."

"Do you think the story of the other missing women out of Saint Ignace connects to Sarah? Something's happening that someone desperately wants to cover up, is what I think," Willis speculates.

"If I hear anything around town, I'll stop in and give you an update. I drive down this street all day. It's the only way to get to where I want to go," Bob says.

"I always see you in your truck with your dog passing by my windows. You must have the daily routes you take around the village."

"I try to keep busy, or I'll just be slowly dying, bored at home. I might not get paid to watch over this town anymore, but I still enjoy taking my old route with my dog, Malko, and Mike for some of it. The drive helps remind us about better times in Newberry. With that crazy killer roaming around, things could get pretty quiet around town. I'm not much of a religious man, but I say a prayer just in case someone is listening. Not giving up on finding Sarah is our most effective weapon against whoever is behind the recent missing people in the area. I've seen plenty of wild things around these northern woods, including past cases of missing people. Honestly, it has never turned out how we wanted it to, and that's a shame. I hope I'm wrong and things change this time with Sarah. Around eight years ago or so, we found a floating body weeks after a man named Mark Gladwell vanished at the Dollarville Dam without a trace. Some guys were fishing, and the man's body floated like a raft toward the fishing pier. The autopsy reported it as a self-inflicted gunshot. From what I saw on the body when they loaded it up on the ambulance at the scene; it didn't look self-inflicted, but the family chose to have the body incinerated at Porter Funeral Home before I could view it myself. I think the out-of-town investigators just didn't want to waste their time. It still rubs me the wrong way that his family is walking around this area and still thinks he took his own life. I even spoke to his wife, Nancy, about my concerns, but she didn't seem interested. I've got to check on my dog before he tears up my truck. Hopefully, I'll be back this afternoon with good news for you."

"I hope so, Bob. Thanks again for looking out for us. It might not seem like much to you, but it makes the area feel safer knowing someone is looking out for us all."

"After all these years, I've still got a sharp aim even from my truck window," Bob says with a giant smile and a wink, tipping his Carhartt hat as he walks out of Northern Bites. Willis looks on through the windows of the café as Malko, Bob's dog, barks at him from the half-rolled-down window of his truck, happy to see his owner on his way.

CHAPTER 15

Bob was spot on about the quiet morning traffic flow as the morning moved slowly for Willis without customers. Willis tried to keep busy cleaning and organizing with periodic glances out Northern Bites' windows. He hoped Bob would return through the doors with good news of the killer being caught or Sarah returning home, but nothing happened. While taking inventory, Willis hears the front door chime, meaning a customer has finally decided to come in or Bob has some news, but instead Willis sees Larry walking into the bakery. As long as Larry is around, Willis's mornings should go quickly now that he has someone to talk to, so he can keep his mind busy. Larry has exciting stories or news that could be borderline conspiracy theories involving people in Luce County, the government, or Viking culture.

"Good morning, Willis. The usual, my friend," Larry says, hanging up his jacket and scarf while cleaning the snow off his boots on the entrance mat. "Winter's not settling down yet. Outside, the winter gods seem to still be angry over something we did. A big, nasty storm cell is coming tonight from over by Green Bay. If we get half the snow the meteorologists say we are expecting, we will plow out most of the day tomorrow. Lake Superior can play tricks on us. Sometimes the big lake can drop double what you would expect, but sometimes the snow falls apart over the lake and we get nothing, so it's anyone's guess on what we get."

"Hey Larry, you're testing me, aren't you? You have two favorite orders. Would you like a Cheese Danish, Earl Grey tea, and a splash of cream, or do you want a cinnamon roll with a large mocha? Am I right?" Willis asks, waiting to hear what Larry would like.

"You passed the test with flying colors; well done, my boy. Mocha and a cinnamon roll it shall be. Slow morning around here." Larry asks, walking towards the counter and looking around at the empty bakery.

"So far today, you, Bob, Mike, and my son Archer running around the empty bakery for a while are the only ones. If every day was like this, I might have to work in my father-in-law Ted's sawmill to pay the bills," Willis says while putting maple syrup on Larry's cinnamon roll.

"I don't think Ted would hire you at his sawmill. Running a chainsaw isn't your thing, but you make a decent mocha, so you should stick with Northern Bites. It's off-season, so most places are closed until late spring. I'm sure glad you're not one of those snowbirds that leave us until the grass turns green. For a Saturday, the town seems quieter than usual; perhaps the storm moving in has people already hunkering down."

"Yeah, or maybe it's from what they heard on the news; you heard about the Dirty Elk, right?" Willis asks.

"The Dirty Elk?" Larry asked, looking at Willis, confused.

"Last night, someone shot up The Dirty Elk, with multiple people injured and one person killed. The killer got away and is somewhere between Newberry and Gould City if he didn't make it below the bridge or over into Wisconsin already."

"People being killed around here is another level; even for The Dirty Elk, this is what happens when you cut your local law enforcement. One of the hardest blows our village has recently suffered was the cut to our village police, thanks to the village council. All these issues are because the council can't even tie their shoes, let alone make the right decisions. My dad would roll over in his grave if he could see what they were doing to this area and the old asylum."

"Was your dad involved in local politics around Newberry?" Willis asked.

"Not by choice. My father tried not to be involved with anything other than his job, which never had an off switch, running the state hospital for thirty-five years."

"I never knew your father ran the old state hospital," Willis responds.

"He ran the state hospital until the day it closed. My father had nothing to do with the state hospital's closing, though some locals tried to blame him for it shutting down, but it was all politicians in Lansing. Medical treatment was changing, and places like the state hospital needed to find a new purpose or risk becoming extinct. My father fought hard to save the jobs and for something to come in to replace them if they had to be permanently closed. The Porters, especially Thomas Porter, who was just starting to gain power in the area after his father passed away, tried to bury my family's name. Nothing, and I mean nothing, happens around here without his input."

"How can one person have so much power in a small town?" Willis asks, grabbing a seat next to Larry at his table after bringing him his food and drink.

"Just look around as you drive down Newberry Avenue. The Porters own half the businesses in this town. It didn't take many generations till the Hughes name started to disappear and the Porters kept expanding, popping out kids left and right. Now that Thomas Porter runs the family, it's really taking a turn for the worse; that man just loves power. Thomas Porter and my dad never got along. Most locals viewed my father as the one saving the area. I guess Thomas hated him for getting the recognition instead of his family. It was tough growing up in Newberry for me because of the Porters and Hughes. Most people think I had it easy, but the Porter kids running six generations deep always treated me like an outsider, even though I was born right here in Newberry at Helen Newberry Joy Hospital. After high school, I had to get away for a while. When I graduated from college, I wanted to return, but with the state hospital closed, I felt lost and disconnected. When my father passed away, the Porters influence just grew and grew. So, when I came back to the area, I was the echo of my father's voice, and they hate that. So many people are part of the bloodline of the Hughes or Porters in this town now. You're lucky your wife thought to look outside this small genetic pool; she could've become one of them."

"I might have to ask Ted about the marriages of his grandparents when they immigrated from Finland to this area. Ted has an incredible memory, almost photographic."

"That would be a blessing and a curse, remembering the past, the good moments, as well as the hard times. I have a secret recipe for homemade moonshine for the memories I want to forget, at least temporarily. You should try my moonshine sometime; it works well."

"If things keep going the way they are, I might need to drop by and try some sometime," Willis responds with a chuckle.

"I'm building something; I want to show you when it's completed. So I'll have to have you over as a guest then. Speaking of secret recipes, I have to tell you that last fall, I brought home two loaves of pumpkin bread from here and did everything I could to break it down, and I just couldn't crack the code. What do I have to pay you for the secret recipe price?" Larry asks.

"Joy and her mom are the only ones that know what's in it," Willis replies.

"Speaking of the devil," Larry says as Joy walks in the room.

Hearing Larry's unwelcoming greeting, Joy stares at him disapprovingly.

"Apologies, that was just a figure of speech. Joy, you are an angel sent from the heavens, saving us all from eating the shipped-in grocery store baked goods. Nothing beats fresh baking, and you are Newberry's baking savior," Larry says, lowering himself to the ground and bowing at Joy sarcastically.

"I wouldn't take it that far, but I'll take all the compliments I can get. Willis gets all the accolades, but the actual work is done back in the kitchen. Which recipe were you trying to figure out?" Joy asks.

"The pumpkin bread. I just can't figure it out," Larry says.

"Oh, I see," Joy responds, contemplating if she should give Larry a big hint at the secret recipe.

"I can see you are thinking about it; just tell me the secret recipe. I will promise, in blood, I won't tell another soul," Larry responds with his hands in a prayer position.

"I bet you need more molasses. Is it too dry?" Joy asks.

"It is. I bet that's it," Larry responds with excitement in his voice.

"Something else you didn't know about Joy is that she's not only a gifted baker but also a talented painter. I'm trying to convince Joy to put some of her paintings up for sale on the walls," Willis says.

"If your art is half as good as this cinnamon roll, you have another hit on your hands. Speaking of hits, I'm working on a secret project. Do you want to know what it is?" Larry asks Joy and Willis.

"Sure, but it won't be a secret project anymore," Joy responds sarcastically.

"I trust you two. Have you ever heard of Woodhenge?" Larry asks.

"I know about Stonehenge, but I've never heard about a Woodhenge," Willis curiously replies.

Larry goes on to describe his travels across Europe, backpacking for four months. He tells Joy and Willis how much they will fall in love with England and recommends a trip to London for the whole family. As Larry shares story after story about his wild European adventures, he focuses on a certain part of Stonehenge called Woodhenge that caught his eye. He shares how no one talks about Woodhenge, which is ironic since it's even older than Stonehenge. Larry shares that a replica of it in the northern woods of the Upper Peninsula would be a fascinating way to pay tribute to his nomadic ancestors. Larry then mentions that a few weeks ago he bought a beautiful piece of land next to the former state hospital, which he plans to build his own Woodhenge on. To do the project justice, Larry plans to recreate an exact replica meticulously, not sparing any expense, and then offer it free to the public. Larry tells Willis and Joy he was inspired to make it happen after seeing what they did, giving new life to the Newberry Building with the bakery. The conversation excites Larry enough to start the planning stages for the project for the spring and map out a perfect location on the five-acre lot that very day. After putting on his jacket and scarf and opening the front door to leave Northern Bites, Larry turns around and tells Willis not to forget to talk to Ted about any family ties to the Hughes and Porter families and to visit the Newberry library to learn more about the past histories of those families and Newberry.

As the workday is coming to a close, Willis is ready for the slow day to end, with the town on edge over a killer on the loose. The slow end of the day gives Willis way too much time to think. As Willis is about to start the closing list for the day, he hears the chime of the front door, with kids laughing and chasing each other as they come into the Northern Bites. An older, gray-haired lady with a cane is helped up the entry step by one of the children as another holds the entry door open for her. While the kids look around the room, Willis notices the lady has an eye patch as she looks over the menu. While helping her decide what the kids would like, Willis realizes this lady is similar to what Neal described of the recently released drug dealer known as Mother Mary. If this is who Neal described, she looks nothing like someone who could be a threat to the village at her old age, at least anymore. The years look like they have taken an intense toll on her, as she can hardly walk even with that cane. As she looks over the menu and the fresh pastries at the displays, Willis looks into the cash drawer at the business card Neal gave him to contact him if he ever saw her in town.

"I would like three vanilla frappuccinos, four brownies, and a green tea for myself," says the old lady, with three children asking for treats.

Willis gives the lady her total, and she pulls out a stack of bills from her purse, giving Willis $50, and says to put the rest in the tip jar, giving Willis a smile.

"I haven't seen you in here before; are you visiting family here in Newberry?" Willis asks.

"I used to live here, but I'm moving back to town. I've been away for too long. I missed these little ones so much while I was away. I'm so glad you did something different with the Newberry Building. When I was a kid, this place drew people from hours away to eat at the restaurant and stay the night. My family had a clothing store right across the street. I'm glad to see you trying to bring this old building back to life, giving these kids somewhere to go," the old lady says as she kisses one of the children's heads.

Willis cleaned up after the orders, looking over at the old lady, wondering how this lady could cause so much pain to this community. Many times, Willis had imagined Mary to be far different than she appeared. Willis pondered how a woman who looked like a gust of wind could knock her down posed such a large threat to the community.

Willis rushed to the back kitchen and gestured for Joy to join him in the back prep area, away from Mary and the children, so he could share what was going on with her privately.

"I could tell it was slow since Larry left; I only heard the door chime once. I thought maybe it was Bob or someone coming in to give you the latest on the fugitive," Joy says.

"I need to tell you something," Willis whispers to Joy.

"What?" Joy asks quietly.

"An undercover agent named Neal mentioned that an old lady who used to run the local drug ring in Newberry was getting out of prison, and this lady matches how he described her."

"That's crazy. She has to be as old as my father or maybe my grandmother," Joy says, peeking around the corner to take another look at the lady.

"It's hard to believe, but that's exactly how Neal described her. Maybe she is somehow connected to the killer on the loose," Willis says quietly.

Willis and Joy continued to chat in the back of the bakery when they heard the front door chime. They looked back around the corner into Northern Bites and saw the children helping Mary out of the front door. Willis and Joy watched through the window as Mary walked down the street slowly with her grandchildren's help.

"I'm going to give Neal a call right now to let him know Mary is back in town," Willis says to Joy while typing in Neal's number on his cellphone.

"I slept in way too late this morning, so I'm way behind on the soups. You seemed restless during the night; I kept waking up with all your tossing and turning last night and heavy breathing on me." Joy says as she stands by Willis as he calls Neal and leaves a voicemail detailing the presence of the lady, similar in appearance to Mother Mary, who visited the bakery with her grandchildren.

"According to what I heard from Bob this morning, the state police found the man's truck in Curtis this morning at a boat launch."

"Thanks for waiting till this morning to share; he's still on the loose If you had told me last night, I would have stayed up all night worrying and not slept well.

"Do you hear that?" Willis asks, listening intently.

"Hear what?" Joy responds, not hearing anything.

"I think I heard someone shoveling out back," Willis says, standing silently until they both hear the sounds of a shovel scraping through the wall on the backside of the building.

Willis and Joy walk to the back door of the building, unlocking the door, and see Ted out back, shoveling their walkway clear.

"It sounds like a lot of new snow is possibly falling tonight, so I cleared off the back part of the roof for you. These snow loads seem to refreeze with the rain, which makes them heavy. I didn't want your roof to collapse. You have your work cut out to restore this old historic landmark. The last thing you need is another hassle," Ted says, putting his shovel into the snow banks.

"Thank you for clearing the snow," Willis tells Ted.

Ruth wanted me to invite you all over for dinner, so come on over. I need to deliver maple syrup to Albert's house. I forgot to drop off the syrup yesterday when I stopped at his place, so I'm going to make a stop back home for the maple syrup, quickly drop it off at Albert's, and then head home for dinner," Ted shares.

"Dad, why don't you take Willis to Albert's house while I help Mom get dinner ready? You've been trying to introduce Willis to Albert for years, and you've always wanted to show him around Albert's property," Joy tells Ted.

"That's a great idea. Let's do that. Are you ready for an unforgettable experience at Albert's? Ted asks Willis.

"Sure. You've made Albert's place legendary. Now it's time to see if the stories are all true."

"I'm telling you, my stories don't do Albert's place justice. You'll see for yourself soon enough."

CHAPTER 16

Ted waits patiently for Willis outside his house and fires up his old blue Ford work truck as Willis pulls into his driveway and drops Joy and Archer off with Ruth at Ted's house. While waiting for Willis to come outside, Ted clears off tools and dirt from his passenger seat, making room for Willis. Willis walks out of the house to the truck, holding a large cardboard box filled with glass jars of maple syrup. Ted tells Willis to set the box of syrup in the truck bed and to buckle up for a moment he won't ever forget, seeing Albert's place.

"Didn't you grow up with Albert, Ted?" Willis asks as they travel down the bumpy dirt road to Albert's home.

"I sure did. Al, or Einstein, as I call him, is as close as a brother His family, the Korhonens, were very close to my parents, and we Finnish boys stuck together. We had our own secret language as kids in school. Finnish sounds like gibberish to those who don't understand it. Albert and I got away with saying many things other kids would've gotten suspended for in school. However, no one could tell what we were saying until a guest teacher who was Finnish caught us one day."

"I can't wait to hear more of these stories with you and Al in the same room. I hope we catch Al at home," Willis says.

"Al does not have to tell me he'll be home, because that man never leaves his place." Ted replies.

As the truck turns down the dirt-filled road to Albert's, Willis notices large warning signs on each side of the road. Willis sees a giant yellow crossing sign with a bigfoot walking across a highway, saying 'Bigfoot Crossing' on it, and another road sign says, 'Keep out unless you owe me money'.

"It's all just a joke and an inexpensive security system," Ted says, looking over at Willis.

"If the signs don't scare you off, I bet Al has quite the gun collection waiting on intruders." Willis replies.

"Al hates guns, so no need to worry; you're with me anyway. He is likelier to have a live landmine in his yard than for us to get shot at. Over the years, I helped Al find these signs; my favorite is just ahead. Let me slow down, so you don't miss it."

While driving slowly by the sign, Ted points to the right side of the road. Willis reads the sign: 'Guns don't kill people; I do'.

"The sign still cracks me up after all these years." Ted says, laughing loudly as they slowly pass by the sign.

Turning between two large cut-off tree stumps, the dirt driveway is surrounded by multiple piles of old vehicles and leftover lumber, looking like a personal salvage yard. Ted slows down, letting Willis soak it all in.

"What do you think so far?" Ted asks.

"You have to be kidding me. Albert owns a DeLorean just like the one in *Back to the Future*?" Willis responds stunned, seeing a DeLorean lying half-covered under a blue tarp next to a scrap metal pile.

"It's the same model as the one from the movie; I remember when Einstein bought it in the late 1980s. He is a big fan of that film, especially the character, Doc."

"Is that a tank I see in that part of that pile over there?" Willis asks.

"Part of one, I think. Einstein even has a piece of a submarine somewhere in one of these piles. The Navy was testing the submarine at one point out on Lake Michigan."

"Look at all those old gas station signs! Pickers would have a field day in here," Willis says, staring at a massive pile of rusted Mobilgas signs.

"Yeah, tons of those lying around. Every time a gas station changed signs around town, people viewed them as garbage, but not Einstein. He offered them a few bucks, but mostly local businesses gave them to him for free to get rid of them. Einstein was before his time. Rumors of what he had accumulated spread as treasure hunters really took off with that show *American Pickers*; that's part of the reason for all those warning signs on the property. Those that make it past the signs might come home with some priceless treasures if Einstein is in the mood to sell that day," Ted shares as they drive.

"Did Al build a small fort? Willis asks. looking at the wooden structure up ahead.

"Nope, that's Einstein's place. He built this place himself from pieces of those old Finnish homes left behind in town," Ted replies.

"How did this pass building codes? This place looks like it will fall over with the next decent storm."

"It's been standing for over forty years. Al has used tons of duct tape and some engineering skills to keep that place up during storms. The house looks better than it has in the past," Ted replies. "That's almost impossible to imagine," Willis replies, seeing parts of a tarp tied down to rotted boards swinging back and forth in the wind.

"Here we are; this is Einstein's place. Just wait till you see the inside," Ted says as he pulls in and turns off his pickup truck, parking it in front of the home.

"You're kidding me, Ted. No way someone lives there, right?" Willis asks in shock, as the place looks even worse the closer you get.

"I told you my stories didn't cover the extent of Einstein's place; you must see it to believe it," Ted says, getting out of the truck, then reminding Willis he had to roll down the window and pull the latch from the outside to get out of the truck.

Willis walks up to the house behind Ted, who knocks on the front door three times. Someone can be seen moving throughout the house through openings in the wood walls and door with an eye-catching view of who was outside before they responded.

"Is that Paul Bunyan at my door?" a loud voice shouts from the other side of the door to Ted.

"It is," Ted responds with a chuckle.

After a brief silence, the voice inside the house responds, "What's the secret password?"

It reminded Willis of the wizard in the emerald city scene in the movie *The Wizard of Oz.*

"I brought maple syrup and a special guest," Ted responds, with Willis looking over at him with a puzzled expression as Ted holds up two bottles of maple syrup in the air with a smile on his face.

"That's what I'm talking about; get in here. I just put on a pot of tea," Einstein says from inside the house.

Ted tries twisting the handle twice to open Einstein's front door, but the door won't open.

"Remember to lift up the dang door, Ted. It gets you every time," Einstein yells from inside the house.

"I always forget that. After all these years, you would think I wouldn't have trouble with the door. Maybe WD40 or old motor oil could fix it. When will you get that door fixed?" Ted asks Einstein

"It's not a problem for me; you just need to know what you're doing with it. The bottom sometimes drags, so you have to pull up depending on how much water is in the soil," Einstein says with one hand on a steaming tea kettle.

Willis looked around the home, absorbing every last detail as if time had slowed down. The home's ceiling is made of a mix of rusted metals, magazines, Amazon boxes, and blue tarps, and the floors are made of dirt instead of hardwood or carpet. Orange buckets are located systematically all around the house to catch drips from the ceiling that make it through the home's half-tarped, rusted metal roofing sheets. Magazine stacks, glass jars, and old metal coffee cans cover every inch of the counter space and tables in the kitchen area. The only small window letting in light comes from above the kitchen sink, with one flickering light bulb dangling in the center of the kitchen.

Willis looked for a place to sit with Ted in the kitchen and heard a grunt. He glances to his left and sees a woman wearing a pink house robe and white furry slippers. She is watching television in a recliner with dirt floors and power cords openly running across the ground. The only thing covering the dirt floor in the room with the lady was an antique-looking burgundy Victorian rug underneath the recliner. The woman notices Willis looking over, waving hello, and gives him a friendly smile as he walks by the doorway.

"Hi," Willis says to the lady in the recliner.

"That's my wife, Julie; you caught us watching *Jeopardy*," Einstein says.

"Einstein, this is Willis, whom I've told you about," Ted says to Einstein, with Einstein reaching out a hand to give Willis a handshake.

"Nice to meet you, Willis. All I've heard from Ted over the years is good things; other than that, you're not a logger like Ted here." Einstein says.

"I would've cleaned up a bit if I knew you were coming by; let me clear you off a couple of seats," Al says, moving stacks of books from the coffee table chairs and wiping off the seats with his hand.

"Are you a green tea fan?" Einstein asks Willis.

"I'd love to have a cup." Willis says as Einstein brings over a tea bag and a hot cup of water, handing them to Willis.

"Vermont, it's Vermont, Julie!" Einstein shouts, hearing the question on *Jeopardy* from the kitchen to his wife. I can't believe how long it takes some people to figure out the answers on *Jeopardy* nowadays. Years ago, people seemed to give me a challenge on this show, but none of these young guns impressed me other than Ken Jennings. I only beat him twice to the answers."

"So how did you get the nickname Einstein, by the way? Ted says he's always called you that," Willis asks.

"Ted is the only one who calls me that. Ted can tell the story better than I can," Einstein says, looking over at Ted.

"One might think that Albert Einstein earned his name in high school because he excelled in school or was valedictorian of his class, which he was. However, the name actually came from how he would act in class, sit at his desk, finish his assignment, and then abruptly leave school in the middle of class, sometimes to the teachers and fellow students' surprise. Also, he never cared how he dressed. In those days, schools were really strict on what you would wear to class, and Einstein would show up with his shirt untucked, covered in dirt, baggy pants, and his mom's house slippers on. Nothing's changed; just look at him," Ted sarcastically says, looking over at Einstein, still dressing as messy as he did in high school.

"The school was lucky I even bothered to put on pants before coming to class," Einstein shares. Most of the time, I don't look at what I wear. I just grab whatever is closest to me in the dark and go.

Julie says, from the recliner, hearing the conversation in the other room.

"One of a kind," Ted replies.

"Remember how much we despised high school? Your parents would drag you in," Einstein says to Ted.

"Why would I want to be enslaved in that prison instead of being out in the real world, making money? It's not easy to sit by when you already know what you want to do," Ted replies.

"You sound like my son, Archer. When we take him to preschool, he loves socializing and playing games, but he tells us the schoolwork is too simple, and he's just turned five," Willis says to Einstein, who walks over, sitting down behind a computer on a small desk with stacks of magazines and clutter around it.

"He has good genes," Einstein responds, laughing, pulling down his glasses, and looking at his computer screen. "You can't win them all. I just lost seven thousand dollars, Ted."

"Day trading again?" Ted asks.

"Yeah, some penny stocks I've been following. I made twenty-four thousand yesterday, so it's not a big deal; I'll get it back tomorrow or the next day. It's more fun than anything." Einstein says to Willis' amazement

"I should put my money with you, Einstein," Ted says from his chair at the coffee table.

"Ah, I don't touch other people's cash. I have plenty of money to play with on my own. I have to do something fun with it," Albert says.

"Einstein here in the 1970s developed a lug nut and sold the patent to the Air Force, and they are still using it today," Ted tells Willis.

"I could have built the biggest home in Luce County years ago, but this is all I've ever needed or wanted. My home. doesn't have indoor plumbing. Except for this sink. If you need to use the restroom, it's outside. You can see it from the window," Einstein says, pointing out the window with Willis getting up from his chair for a look.

Willis looked out the window and saw Al's bright blue outhouse.

"Julie was complaining about our old one, so I upgraded that a couple of years ago. You should see the old one," Einstein says, washing dishes by hand. "No need for the mess inside; when that outhouse works just fine, other than when it's a blizzard, things can get tricky. We are just simple folks, right, honey?" Einstein shouts, waiting for a response from Julie in the other room.

"You betcha," Julie says from the other room, still watching *Jeopardy*.

"Einstein, I wanted to introduce you in person to Willis for starters and pick your brain a bit about these missing people around here and your thoughts on it. I've always respected your unique take on things," Ted shares.

"Tragic, isn't it that these things have reached our peaceful small town?" Einstein comments with a worried look.

"Peace has been elusive for our village for generations, possibly ever since the arrival of the colonizers who displaced the native people from their land. I don't know how the situation in Newberry has escalated to this point or who is involved. However, I can say that the problem originates from within our community rather than from external sources such as drug rings or big cities. Truthfully, I doubt that someone from our village will be able to resolve the problem. Discovering the truth and finding a solution are two different challenges. I suspect that certain individuals in our village know who is involved but are reluctant to speak up for various reasons. The only person who could put an end to this once and for all is someone like you, Willis, an outsider. Don't you have a background in investigation?"

"Investigating community problems, but never criminals."

Ted has bragged about you, mentioning that you have won multiple awards in the past for your reporting in your parents' newspaper and in college.

"That was just a bunch of small town awards. I don't think this is something I can do. I'm just a small-town business owner now, and this is something the FBI or the police should handle."

"The police would've fixed all these drug problems years ago if they could or wanted to. The same philosophy works for this case as any other one you've looked into in the past. They're nothing different from what you've learned than someone would do to discover what's happening in this town. In another life, maybe I would've become a private investigator myself. What's going on around Newberry isn't a problem a gun can solve or a badge, but by digging deep, till you get the truth, no matter the cost. The closer you are to the answer, the more pressure you will feel to stop."

"I'm a big fan of genuine people. You are as authentic as they come. Thank you for your honest opinion; it gives me something to think about," Willis says.

"I've always been and always will be this way. I don't know any other way to be," Einstein says before taking another sip of his tea.

"We'd better get back to my house soon, Willis, or Ruth will kill me for being late to a warm dinner. I'll get the evil eye if I'm not back while the food's still hot," Ted says as he and Willis say goodbye as they stand up and head towards the doorway.

Willis and Ted arrive back at Ted's home and step inside to the beautiful aroma of freshly baked bread, just in time to be set out on the dining room table, with Archer and Joy buttering their rolls and Ruth giving Ted a stern stare.

"I was getting nervous that your food would get cold," Ruth said, putting the food on the dining room table.

"My internal trigger sounded off at Einstein's, so I got us in the truck as fast as possible. I've learned to listen to the voice inside my head and stomach. When both stir, I know it's dinner time."

"Sometimes you don't listen to it, I guess. Remember last week when you were three hours late for lunch? I almost sent out a search party to see if a tree had fallen over on top of you," Ruth says.

"My internal clock still works fine. I was logging across from Walter Duflo's property, and he brought me some maple syrup from his first batch, and we had pancakes at his cabin.

"You never told me that's where you were. No wonder you didn't eat when you got home that night. Before you sit down to eat, can you add more firewood to the stove? I could feel the weather changing when you all came in. There's some bitter cold in the air outside," Ruth says to Ted as she dishes out spaghetti on Archer's plate.

"How was it meeting Al?" Ruth asks.

While sitting down and fixing his dinner plate, Willis said, "The stories are all true. I can see why Ted enjoys hanging out with him." "Dad, Didn't you and Al once run away together?" Joy asks.

"We did. Our parents sent us away for a week to a church summer camp. One afternoon, we skipped out of line for dinner, slipped into the woods, and hitchhiked back to Newberry. The news traveled fast to our parents, and our moms scolded us when we arrived home. I don't remember ever having my mom pull my ears as hard as she did that day, dragging me inside. All Einstein and I could do was think about all the money we were losing, sitting there listening to some old man preach. Our dads understood and helped us get off with our rears still attached. The next day, we were out making money in the woods. Well, enough with my stories for the night. Let's eat so you all can get back to the Newberry Building before this weather starts to turn for the worst. I can already see some flurries out the window. This storm could be one of the toughest we've dealt with this winter."

CHAPTER 17

At four a.m. the following day, the sound of trucks rushing by Willis's bedroom window stirs him awake. Half-awake, he rises from bed and gazes out the bedroom window, partially covered in frost, with the flashing lights of a fire truck reflecting off the glass as it moves away in the distance. As he gets out of bed to look outside, Willis hears another fire truck rolling by fast, heading north of town. Willis attempted to lie back in bed, but he realized that he was too alert to fall back asleep. He steps into his bathroom to get ready quietly as an ambulance roars past his windows, waking up Joy and his son Archer, who snuck into their bed last night. "I was deep in an amazing dream," Joy says softly, rubbing her eyes and trying to relax Archer so he could fall back to sleep. "After I get Archer back to sleep, I'll check Facebook to see if there are updates about what's going on. Maybe it's related to the fugitive who's still on the run."

After getting Archer comfortable, Joy reaches for her phone and checks Facebook, but nothing has happened in town online yet. Cuddling up next to Archer, Joy tells Willis she will try to go back to sleep.

As customers start to trickle into Northern Bites, with the streets cleared of the heavy overnight snow, the sun briefly comes through the clouds. Willis overhears an older gentleman named Marvin, who's part of a weekly meet-up group named The Wisemen. This group of retired locals alternate between their favorite meeting spots,

Northern Bites and McDonald's. The Wisemen have a large list of hot area topics, from politics to local events. Willis listens to them when he has a free moment and chimes in from time to time. "Quite the fire up north, according to my son," says Marvin to the rest of The Wisemen at the table around him.

"What else did he say about fire?" asks one of the wise men.

"It was nothing like what my son had ever seen as a volunteer firefighter. The fire was so strong it took hours to get it under control, and the snowstorm made it even harder, coming in from Lake Superior in spurts. Once the fire department got control of the fire, there was not much left of the vehicle or those inside."

"People were set on fire? What is wrong with this world? Back in my day, we never had problems like this," shares one of the wise men.

"My son said he noticed the smell of gasoline all around them, and they extinguished the smaller fires before tackling the main one, fire, which was still going strong."

Larry, wearing a matching red flannel scarf and a Stormy Kromer hat, a suit with a checkered tie, and Chuck Taylor dress shoes, walks in and hangs up his coat as The Wisemen continue their discussion.

"No matter the weather, you are always dressed to make a statement, Larry," Willis says.

"You never know who you might run into, so you should always dress to impress, is my rule of thumb. Any news on catching the killer yet, or did some wildlife get to him first in the woods?" Larry asks, heading towards Willis at the checkout counter.

"Nothing new unless he was in that fire this morning in Paradise. I had ambulances and fire trucks racing by my windows this morning, and the guys over here were just talking about the latest news up north."

As Larry spoke, he jokingly suggested adding bourbon or whiskey to his coffee and his assistant's, implying it would be a hectic day. As Larry, Willis, and the Wisemen discuss the fire, Mike walks in alone. Since the day Northern Bites opened, Mike has never come in alone without his partner in crime, Bob.

"Where's your better half? Did you two break up?" Willis sarcastically asked.

"Bob's up at that mess up north in Paradise. I bet he wishes he was here instead. Phil from the DNR called him about the fire late last night. He said in his voicemail that Bob left me a voicemail overnight saying that no one else was available and he had to wait for the Michigan State Police and Fire Department to arrive at the accident. Bob will never fully retire from watching over the area; he just stopped being paid for it," Mike responds.

"Quite a mess Bob's got on his hands up in Paradise from what my son told me," says one of The Wiseman's from his table to Mike.

"You got that right. Bob called me back a few hours later with more details in a voicemail. The message said that a sedan was on fire and three people were inside

"You got that right. Bob called me back a few hours later with more details in a voicemail. The message said that a sedan was on fire and three people were inside All three were burned to their bones by the time he arrived. All that anyone could see inside the car were bones by the time they could reach them when the fire finally died down enough. The cell signal is terrible up that way, so I'm still waiting to get a response from the text I sent Bob. Bob is too old to mess around with this stuff. He needs to leave the police work to those getting paid." A frustrated Mike looks at his phone, hoping for a text from Bob.

As everyone in Northern Bites speculates about the fire, more sirens zoom by downtown. This time, there are four to five state police cars and two more ambulances from surrounding counties right behind them. You could hear a needle drop in the room as those inside Northern Bites turned around to watch the action silently out the windows. This was a level of urgency the residents of Newberry hadn't witnessed before. It was obvious to those inside Northern Bites that what was happening up north was much larger than they could ever imagine. Mike breaks the silence in Northern Bites as everyone around him waits for someone to say something or for more emergency vehicles to pass by.

I am going to head home and listen to the police radars for anything, so I better get on the road," Mike spoke up as everyone in Northern Bites stared anxiously out the window, wondering what would happen next.

"That must be almost every officer for at least an hour away in every direction. The last time I saw anything like this here was a couple of years ago with the duck lake forest fires started up by the Two Hearted River. Keep me in the loop on what you hear, Willis. Here's my number," Larry says, writing down his number on a receipt.

"I'll do that. I hope we're making more of this than it is, and Bob gets back to town okay. He's one of the good guys around here," Willis responds.

"Bob will be just fine; it's not his first rodeo, he's built for moments like this It runs in his family, and over the years, that man has witnessed a lot.

Ronald, Bob's father, served as the head of the Newberry police department for decades. His dad was here during some of this town's hardest times. Bob will watch over this small area as long as he breathes. No one will mess with his town without a fight," Larry declares before leaving.

The day dragged on, giving Willis plenty of time to think about who might have been in the car. His biggest fear was that he knew someone involved in the crash, or even worse, that Sarah was in it. Willis wonders how long it would take to get details of what really happened and who was in the fire. As lunchtime arrives, every seat is filled at Northern Bites with a rush Willis hadn't seen since the peak of the fall color tours. With faces visiting the bakery, Willis hadn't seen them since opening day at Northern Bites. The bakery was packed with people meeting in person to talk about the fire. There was barely any room to move, and the conversation was hushed and somber.

"Hey, could you change the radio?" a man sitting with his family at a crowded table asks Willis.

"I can change the song for you or turn it down a little," Willis replies.

"No, what I'm asking is, can you turn the radio to The Eagle? Maybe they have some updates."

Willis recalls that, given the lack of local television stations for hours, the community depends on The Eagle radio station as the go-to source for breaking local news updates and, when needed, classic rock programming. Willis tries to locate the local radio station online, but the station is not available. Instead, Willis took down an ancient radio from the back shelf, which he knew was still functional because it was being used to renovate the bakery area without internet connectivity.

As he turns on the nearby radio station, Willis remarks, "Here we go; I hope this thing still works."

Within minutes of tuning in to the local radio station, a songs cut off by the breaking news theme music on The Eagle. As everyone waited for the update, all conversation came to a halt.

This is breaking news from your trusted local source, The Eagle. We have just received word from the Michigan State Police that anyone planning to travel to Whitefish Point or Paradise today should expect delays on their route. In addition, you might need to turn back because of continuous whiteout conditions from lake effect snow off Lake Superior. North Whitefish Point Road and Highway 123 will be closed to any incoming traffic until further notice due to a serious vehicle fire and possible casualties. Also, the Gould City area is still an active crime scene, so please avoid that area at this time. The shooter at Gould City is still at large, so please stay inside for your safety. For more breaking news updates, listen to your reliable local news source, The Eagle.

There was a flurry of activity in the room after the news update, with people rising from their seats to talk about what they had just heard on the radio.

"You should've yelled for help; that looks like quite the rush. Did they catch the shooter?" Joy said as she walked into the busy room with Archer in her arms. As she put him down, he ran over to greet a child friend.

"I turned on the local radio for breaking news for everyone. The Eagle said that the main roads into and out of Paradise are closed due to a vehicle fire. Paradise is an active crime scene right now. It doesn't sound like the two events are connected, but you never know." Willis shares with Joy now that Northern Bites is now almost empty.

"What is going on around here? Now a car is on fire. Was anyone in it?" Joy asked.

"I have heard from the radio and Mike that three people have died in the fire so far today," Willis replied.

I've been on the phone with my mom and dad several times this morning, but I doubt they've heard about the car on fire up north yet. You know, my mom, she's glued to the television stations waiting for updates. She won't leave her house until they catch this fugitive on the run. My dad is back out in his sawmill, working like usual, much to my mother's displeasure. When she hears this about the three people killed in a fire-burning car, my mom might never come out of her house." Joy tells Willis, leaning up against a door frame.

Willis and his family decide to visit Joy's parents after closing Northern Bites for the day, giving them a place to step away from work and enjoy someone else's cooking. Spending dinners at Joy's parents has become Willis's family's haven, with Joy bringing over day-old pastries for dinner, to Ted and Ruth's delight. Ted always starts dinner with a prayer of thanks. The conversations at the dinner table are pretty routine, with the latest stories from Ted's lumber deliveries or how the day went at Northern Bites, but tonight, things are different. On any other day of the week, the television is never on at dinner time at Joy's parents' house Ted, however, is willing to defy the dinnertime ban by watching the Marquette news tonight because the Gould City killer is still at large and three people have died in a car fire. Although there are occasional news reports about Newberry, this specific story will garner a lot of attention.

Everyone at Ted's house is surprised that the 5 o'clock news only briefly covered the deaths in Paradise and promised more information later.

The next few days passed with only minor updates and speculation. The people of Newberry were still reeling from the fire in Paradise, and the village was starting to fill with rumors. The incident's victims and the suspects behind the fire piqued the curiosity of many residents, despite reports that everyone was safe except for the missing Sarah. The constant wave erosion along the shores of Lake Superior has led many to believe that any evidence of the fire may have been thrown into the lake, where it could be lost forever. Lake Superior, the largest freshwater lake in the world by area, makes it unlikely for anything to wash ashore soon. The forensics team in Sault Ste. Marie has a difficult task ahead of them as they try to gather evidence from the remains of the burned vehicle and bodies. Willis was hoping for Bob's visit to Northern Bites, but there was no sign of Bob or Mike in days.

CHAPTER 18

Three days after the Paradise fire, news travels across social media and around Newberry locals that a forensic report will be released soon, including the names of those killed in the fire. Information from the forensic report, which will soon be released, is quickly spreading throughout the Upper Peninsula because the case has expanded from a local issue to one that affects the entire state of Michigan. At 2 p.m., the Chippewa Sheriff's Department released the forensic report in a statement.

Chippewa Sheriff's Department Statement:

With the help of the Upper Peninsula Forensics team, the Chippewa Sheriff Department identified those we lost in our community earlier this week. Mike Knox, a forty-five-year-old Manistique resident, was recently released from the Newberry Correctional Facility after serving six years. Mr. Knox committed the Gould City murders at The Dirty Elk, which is still under investigation. Paula Fox, age thirty-three, is the woman missing from Saint Ignace, and Newberry resident Sarah Clark, age twenty-eight, has been missing for twenty-three days. The Chippewa Sheriff's Department will release additional information at a later time.

Willis and Joy were reading the report on Facebook together Though it should have been consoling, knowing Sarah's whereabouts and the identity of the Gould City murderer wasn't. Knowing she passed away in a burning car seemed to hurt even more than not having answers. It was devastating knowing Sarah would never be back together with her daughter, Ava, and her fiancé, Noah.

The news story quickly spread across Michigan, dominating news broadcasts and newspaper headlines. Even news outlets in Detroit and Chicago covered the deaths, with the big question on everyone's mind: who was behind it? Locals' phones were lit up with media requesting interviews with anyone who would talk. Some news stations sent field reporters to get in-person interviews with news vans roaming the small-town streets. They asked anyone they saw in the streets if they knew anyone, Sarah.

The reason behind the car fire off the coast of Lake Superior was a mystery to everyone in the region. There was no indication of a connection between the three people discovered inside the flaming automobile, and their deaths seemed senseless. The car looked as though it had caught fire on its own. The only thing the three had in common, despite the state police's best efforts to connect them, was that they had all grown up in the Upper Peninsula. According to accounts, Sarah had never met the other two people. Meth was discovered in the driver's seat of Mike Duggan's truck in Curtis, the Gould City killer who died in the car fire, sparking rumors of drug involvement. Mike Duggan had an extensive criminal history, including previous drug busts and break-ins at homes. There were no records of such activities for Sarah or the other woman in the fire. With Sarah's passing, Ava was torn from her comfortable life and sought solace in the warmth of Chelsea and her mother's house on the reservation. Ava and Chelsea were shielded from media attempts to interview them by the other families in the reservation surrounding them.

Noah is still considered a suspect in the investigation, which prevents him from having any contact with Ava, the girl he raised as his daughter. Noah is not even allowed to visit Ava for her safety, and Chelsea has refused his request for custody, letting the courts decide what's best for Ava. The Michigan State Police and the FBI continue to investigate the cause of the killings, but the case grows colder by the day.

Rumors circulated about who could have committed the act. Mary and Noah were often mentioned as possible suspects. However, there was no evidence linking Noah or Mother Mary to the crime. The rumors were based solely on speculation and hearsay.

After a few weeks, people in Newberry go on with their lives, and Sarah's death gradually disappears from the public eye—even though her murder remains unsolved. Chelsea returns to work following her leave of absence to spend time with Ava and to further process the loss of her best friend. After Chelsea's first day back, she assisted Willis in bringing the dirty dishes to the kitchen's cleaning sinks as Northern Bites closed for the day. Willis decided it would be a good time to see how Chelsea was doing now that she was back at work while he filled the cleaning sinks. "I hope it wasn't too much coming back so soon after everything that's been going on. If you need more time off, just let me know," Willis says to Chelsea while wiping down dishes together.

"I guess I'm doing okay. Having something to do to get my mind off things is good for me. I just wish they would find out why this all happened to Sarah," Chelsea responds while doing dishes.

"I hate to ask, but do you think Noah had anything to do with it?" Willis asks.

"I'm the wrong person to ask. Noah and I never saw eye to eye. I've had too many run-ins with Noah over the years. I never saw what Sarah saw in him until recently. I wanted the best life for Sarah, so I did everything in my power to keep her as far away from him as I could. When Noah gets mad, he can lose his cool and go off the handle. Sarah was never physically harmed, but he would often raise his voice and become emotional. Sarah loved him unconditionally; no matter what he or she did, she always came back to Noah. When Sarah had Ava, I thought that was it between her and Noah, but somehow Ava brought them even closer together." Chelsea shared while taking a break from washing the dishes.

"Till all this happened, I thought Ava was Noah's daughter," Willis responds.

Most people believe that Noah is Ava's dad. Noah's been with Ava her whole life, the only father she's ever known. He stood by Sarah when Ava was born, holding her hand even though Ava wasn't his child. I hate keeping Ava away from Noah, but it's for her safety. No one has seen Noah in weeks." Chelsea says.

"Who's Ava's father then?" Willis asks.

"Sarah drank a little too much at a house party one night and hooked up with a random guy she only saw once and got pregnant while she and Noah were split up. That was the only time Sarah had ever been with anyone other than Noah. Ava's biological father is a real creep. When Sarah told him she was pregnant, the guy just yelled at her over the phone. Days later, she found out why because the guy ended up being married. Even in a small area like this, you still don't know who everyone is. The news got to the guy's wife, which caused quite a mess since she's a Porter. The Porter family tries to maintain a wholesome image, but their behavior suggests otherwise. The guy tried to convince Sarah not to go through with the pregnancy and get an abortion. Sarah and I had some deep talks with plenty of tears, and in the end, she decided to have Ava. The guy wanted nothing to do with Ava, giving up custody of her and spreading rumors that the baby was really Noah's. He even said Sarah slept around with everyone in town, so no one really knows who the father really is. One night, Noah went to get a drink at a bar and decked the guy after he made some harsh comments about Sarah, knocking him out with one punch. That's one moment I really liked and respected Noah. Ava has brought out a softer side in Noah over the last couple of years. He seemed like a changed man, motivated to better himself."

"I know he was trying hard to build a business for his family. All he did was talk about Ava and Sarah when he was here working." Willis shares.

"I have a couple of drawings Ava made for Noah of the three of them together. Could you give him those?" Chelsea asks.

"For sure, next time I am out, I will drop those at Noah's. I need to check in on him."

"It is not just a case; learning what happened to Sarah and the others is like having a piece of our hearts torn out. Please do not stop digging and fighting so that we can discover the truth."

CHAPTER 19

Willis decided to follow up on Larry's suggestion to explore the history of Newberry at the local library. He believed that despite any efforts to erase history, it could never be truly forgotten. So one afternoon, he went to the library to find out more about the history of Newberry. There will always be those who remember, and there will always be a record of what happened. Willis walked down to the Newberry Library, which was located at Newberry High School. Combining the public and school libraries saved the community money, a common practice in small communities across Michigan's Upper Peninsula. As Willis entered the front door, he saw Rob, the librarian, waving hello.

Rob is a tall man with a long, scraggly beard, standing at least six feet, six inches. Rob was not your typical librarian. He didn't dress like one, and his taste in music was far from what you might expect. He had a well-built physique, suggesting lifting heavy weights daily. He preferred ACDC over Bach, but that didn't mean he lacked intelligence. His brain was a powerhouse, capable of retaining vast amounts of information and dispensing it at lightning speed. In short, don't judge a book by its cover. Rob recently took over as the librarian, coming from outside Bad Axe, Michigan. He fell in love with the northern woods around Newberry a few summers ago at an Iron Man event. The news of the librarian's impending retirement stirred a dormant restlessness in Rob. He pictured himself amidst the towering shelves, the scent of aged paper a familiar comfort, a new start in the heart of Newberry.

"Welcome Willis, The last time I saw you here, you hooked us on the samples you dropped off. You are welcome to bring them again any time." Rob says it with a chuckle.

"I learned that quickly dropping off samples would be one of the most effective tricks for increasing business. Speaking of tricks, what's the best trick to examine the area's history here at the library?" Willis asks.

"You are in for a treat. We have some fabulous local self-published books, all about the beginning of Newberry to the present, in our regional section, but if you ask me, they are just snapshots. I would recommend looking at the newspaper archives if you really want to see the past."

"How far back do the archives go?" Willis asks with piqued interest.

"All the way back. One of the first things opened in Newberry was the newspaper; it's like a time machine. Now and then, I'll take a peek back into a certain period for fun. It's amazing how some things change and others stay the same over time."

"That sounds like what I need," Willis says.

Rob walks Willis to a small side room.

"Have you ever used a microfilm machine?" Rob asks, looking at Willis standing next to the microfilm machine.

"Maybe once in grade school as a requirement before computers took over everything."

"Despite not being a popular tool any more, microfilm is still one of the most valuable resources available to learn about the past. A couple of decades ago, this was the place to find everything you needed. Now, with the internet, you can just click on a search engine and get what's online, but so much of what's on microfilm here locally isn't online yet, so this is the only way to find it. Most students don't even know this microfilm exists. Some use it for class history projects for a couple of weeks, but that's about it. The depth of information is unbelievable on this microfilm. It can take some time to get used to this machine, but whatever you're looking for, this is your best chance of finding it. These records go all the way back to 1882."

"Starting at the beginning sounds like the right place to start," Willis responds.

Rob opens a metal filing cabinet drawer and pulls out a sealed container with the microfilm inside, handing it gently to Willis.

"Make sure to keep your hands off the film, which could damage it. Not even the newspaper's archives have all these, especially the oldest papers. I want to digitize these myself sometime soon, just in case anything should happen to the originals. If, let's say, a fire happened, a vast amount of priceless Upper Peninsula history would be lost forever. Let me load the first one for you; then you should have the hang of it," Rob says, showing Willis how to handle the film and adjust the viewer before he walks out of the room and back to the information desk. Willis bends down and adjusts the viewer to sharpen the image. Viewing the microfilm, Willis immediately feels like he has stepped back in time with the image.

Willis looked over his notebook to find specific dates of events he had heard mentioned by Ted and Larry. As he looks through the pages, he's stunned by drastic changes in the prices of goods and the language used to describe people, which would lead to lawsuits today. Willis scratched off dates in his notebook, searching through different microfilms one by one. Nothing stands out as different from what the locals have told Willis until he reaches the founding fathers of the Vulcan Furnace Company. The Vulcan Furnace Company was the first industrial company to move into Newberry, specializing in iron smelting, logging, and farming. Under the headline image, Willis saw a name he had never heard mentioned before: Isaac Bernard. Isaac Bernard was standing in the black-and-white picture next to the man from whom Newberry received its name, John S. Newberry, in Detroit. In the story below the pictures, it states Isaac Bernard was the first supervisor hired by John Newberry, with no mention of Mr. Hughes or Mr. Porter in the article. All the stories shared with Willis stated that John Newberry never even visited Newberry but helped establish Newberry from his mansion in Detroit. Willis continues reading the article, talking about Isaac Bernard moving to Newberry from the Corktown area of Detroit to supervise the building of the Vulcan plant. With these new revelations, Willis stops and writes down the details as quickly as possible, realizing he's on to something.

Willis focuses on the next few weeks of the newspaper archives on microfilm, searching through all the slides with no luck of any follow-up on Isaac Bernard until five months later in the obituary section. The story was a brief write-up, listing the names of his wife and children, and then mentioning Isaac's bravery in helping save two others from a log pile collapse at a delivery station in the small town next to Newberry called Dollarville. Willis writes down the family members' details and the date of Isaac's death in his notebook.

Out of curiosity, Willis continues to look through the following week's newspapers, finding Samuel Porter and Paul Hughes taking over the position of joint supervisors of the Vulcan plant.

Making inroads on his research, Willis looks over at what's left on his notes of things to search for, with only one date not scratched off his list: the closing of the Newberry State Hospital. The Newberry State Hospital shut its doors in the early 1990s after being the center of growth in the area after the logging camp boom ended. Willis finds an article about an organization put together to save the Newberry State Hospital a few years before its closing. The newspaper presented various ideas, such as establishing a community college or a trade school for the extensive grounds of Newberry State Hospital. However, the village council voted down these proposals in a close vote of five to four. The village mayor, James Porter, pursued the safer bet of turning the Newberry State Hospital into a correctional facility with state funds. In the article, Willis reads about Larry's father, Ronald Burke. Minutes later, while deep in thought reading an article on the last child of the Hughes passing on and his business being sold to the Porters, Willis feels a hand tap him on his right shoulder, startling him.

"Sorry to spook you, Willis. Did you get lost in time?" Rob asked, "I just wanted to let you know the library's closing in ten minutes, but feel free to finish up. I still have books to check in and return to the shelves."

Willis gathered his notes after spending three hours looking over microfilm. He had pages of notes to follow up on, but before heading home, he jotted down one last thought: he needed to ask Ted about Isaac Bernard.

After spending way more time than expected at the library, Willis drives over to Ted's house, hoping not to show up late to dinner.

"What were you doing at the library for three hours?" Joy asks.

"I thought the library would only take an hour, but I found out way more than I would imagine looking through old microfilms. I got lost in it. I have some questions to ask Ted," Willis says.

Ted walks in a few seconds later from outside, right behind Willis, covered in sawdust shavings from working in his mill, smelling like fresh-cut pine.

"Hey Ted, I know you just got back from working all day out in the mill, but I was just at the library digging up some history on Newberry and have a few questions for you," Willis tells Ted.

"To Ruth's displeasure, a shower can wait for a good conversation about Newberry history. What did you find? Old Bigfoot sightings from the area?" Ted asks, taking off his work flannel jacket and shaking off the sawdust outside the doorway to avoid getting it on the kitchen floor.

"Even better than that, I promise," Willis responds, piquing Ted's interest even more.

"That's hard to believe; you know how much I love a good Bigfoot story. Ted said this while he threw his work shirt in the laundry hamper

"I went all the way back to the beginnings of Newberry in 1882 in the old newspapers stored on microfilm. While looking through the pages, I found a name I haven't ever heard mentioned about the founders of Newberry, Isaac Bernard. The newspaper said Isaac was the original manager of the Vulcan plant. Have you ever heard that name before, Ted?" Willis asks.

"I've seen a lot of people come and go in Newberry over the years, but that's one name I don't recall ever hearing." Ted replies.

"Isaac Benard died during a log pile collapse incident in Dollarville just months after taking the project management position. The next time I get a chance, I'll print out the old paper if I can from the microfilm in the library."

"You know, now that I think of it, I'm familiar with a few Bernards that used to live in town." Ted replies.

Willis shares more about looking into the beginnings of Newberry. He shows Ted the notes from searching on the microfilm, digging around into the last years of the Newberry State Hospital, showing how tough and contested that closing was on Newberry.

"Seeing that hospital close on the last day was one of the saddest days of my life, but I'm glad they at least did something by putting the prison in its place. The biggest part that still stings is all those beautiful old buildings sitting vacant next to the prison, just wasting away. I sometimes wonder as I drive by the hospital grounds what could've been if we did something else with those state hospital grounds. These days, you can't even step beyond the fences unless you're a prison inmate or a correctional officer. When I was a kid, we would ride our bikes freely around the Newberry State Hospital all the time. How I wish I could show you, Joy, and Archer what it looked like back when I was young. Even after decades of decay, if we could walk around those amazing buildings today, you would still feel how special they are."

"Ted, you would've loved those old microfilms. Looking at those old newspapers is like jumping back into time at any point in Newberry's history," Willis shares.

"Oh, don't tell Ted that. I'll never get him to cut logs in the mill now. Instead of being in the sawmill, he'll be down at the library every day digging up the past instead of making money," Ruth says, jokingly, cleaning up some messes on the table Archer left behind from dinner.

"Now wait a minute, Ruth, hear me out. I promise to keep the fireplace burning and my customers happy, but it would be fun, maybe from time to time, to look at some of those moments. I'll still be your Paul Bunyan, don't you worry, honey," Ted says, moving toward Ruth in the kitchen, acting like he's going to give her a hug with a giant smile on his face.

"Don't you dare get one more step closer. Get down to the shower in the basement right now, then maybe you'll get that hug; you're filthy," Ruth says, taking a step back from Ted with a finger pointing at him.

"I'll make my way to the shower in the basement, but before I head down to the dungeon, the name was Isaac Bernard, right?" Ted asks Willis.

"Yes, Isaac Bernard," Willis replies.

"I want to look more into that mystery man, Mr. Bernard, myself. I have a large collection of books covering the early years of Newberry. I'll look over my books again tonight to see if I overlooked that name in the past. If I can't find anything about Isaac Bernard, maybe we can stop by the Luce County Museum," Ted says.

"Isn't the museum closed for the year till late spring?" Willis asks.

"I know people. I'll get us in," Ted says, looking over at Willis with a grin before heading down into the basement.

CHAPTER 20

After reviewing his historical books on Newberry and finding nothing about Isaac Benard, Ted calls Paul, the head historian for the Newberry Historical Society Museum. Paul is thrilled to give Willis and Ted a private tour, as it's been months since the museum last opened its doors to guests.

As Ted pulls up in front of the History Museum, he warns Willis.

"I've met Paul numerous times at events, and this young man can talk your ear off. No one knows more about this town than that young man, not even me."

Paul, a skinny, middle-aged man with brown hair and dark-rimmed glasses, meets Willis and Ted at the front steps of the Luce County Museum.

"Welcome! Have you been here before Willis?" Paul asked..

"Once with my son Archer, which turned into a brief visit. My son's only four, so he enjoyed acting like a criminal in the old jail cell on the top floor, so that's where I spent most of my time."

"I once spent the night in that cell," Ted says, with Willis and Paul looking at him in shock.

"What? You've never shared that story, and I thought I had heard everything," Willis responds.

"I'm only kidding, but I wonder what it would be like to spend the night in a jail cell and what the free food's like," Ted replies.

"Well, let's hope you never find out," Paul said jokingly. "The heat's been turned down to a minimum for months, so there could be a cold chill in the rooms."

As they walk through the museum doors, Ted soaks in the history, looking around the Victorian-styled room that looks like the old living room area. Ted took a deep breath and closed his eyes. He could smell the history all around him. The musty scent of old books, the faint hint of wood smoke. He opened his eyes and looked around the room.

"Since the jail closed in the early 1950s, the caretakers of the building have tried to keep the old Victorian feel of this building. At one time, this floor was the home of the sheriff," Paul tells Willis and Ted as they look around the room.

Ted pulled out his reading glasses from his jacket pocket and bent down to examine the pages of an old book. He held the pages of the book up to his nose and inhaled deeply, savoring the musty scent of history.

"Joy smells the pages like that," Willis says, watching Ted smell the old book pages.

"I taught her well then," Ted says, taking one last big sniff before setting down the book with something else, drawing his attention to the other side of the room.

"Look right here. Oh, these were the golden days of Newberry and this country," Ted says, holding up a black-and-white picture with people dancing in the downtown streets laughing in the image. "Oh, how I wish I could be back in the 1960s again. Just look at how happy those people look; all those filled downtown storefronts are bustling behind them. I remember, as a young boy, bringing newspapers to some of these stores. My favorite place to visit was the candy shop at the bottom of the Newberry Building. The lady running the register would always let me pick out something from the penny candies for free," Ted shares, reminiscing.

I'm envious you got to live during those times, Ted. Newberry was a thriving village. The state hospital was flourishing, and the lumberyards couldn't hire enough people," Paul replies, looking over Ted's shoulder at the image.

"Speaking of the state hospital, would you have anything that shows the old layout that Ted and I could look at? Ted's always sharing with me how his mother worked at the hospital in the old theater building, and he wanted to show me what the place was like inside since we can't go into the grounds," Willis asks Paul.

"We haven't created a dedicated area for the state hospital yet, but we should, with so many images and historical documents for it. I think I have exactly what you need back in storage; let me go grab it," Paul says before leaving the room.

"Look here," Ted says to Willis, pointing at an old image on a shelf. Willis notices the photo is of a group of old loggers standing on top of a massive pile of logs in the woods, smoking cigarettes and cigars.

"Here we go," Paul says, walking with excitement in his voice with a giant roll of papers in his hands. "Could you both help me for a minute with clearing off this table so we have space to look at what I have to show you?"

"Absolutely," Ted eagerly responds, helping clear off a wooden table.

Paul lays out the papers, unveiling a blueprint in front of Willis and Ted, with the blueprint running from one end of the table to the other. Paul explains that these are the original blueprints from the State of Michigan in 1895. Everything on these plans aligns with what they did with the first stages of the state hospital. This print is one of the only documents to have the original name 'Upper

Peninsula Asylum for the Insane' for the Newberry State Hospital is stamped on the top left corner. The blueprint shows the massive size of the Newberry State Hospital grounds, with thousands of patient rooms filling the long hallways at one point. Paul shares that state hospitals didn't have the greatest reputation around Newberry during its early years. Many protested how people were treated inside the hospital. Overall, the patients needed serious help and were insane, as Paul explained.

"When I was a kid, you could walk into the facility. No fences, just open land for the public to enjoy. Sometimes, I would get bored at home and head over to the theater building on my bike, drop my bike on the grass right outside the back entrance, and sneak up onto the balcony to watch the movies with the inmates. The popcorn and movie selection were great. Over the years, I learned the ins and outs of sneaking my way anywhere on those grounds without a parent's guidance. Some people in the state hospital truly were crazy, but with most, you could hold a conversation. The terrible cases never left the buildings deep in the complex," Ted shared while looking over the blueprint intently. chuckled, pointing at the theater building.

"Is that right, the Newberry State Hospital grounds cover 750 acres?" Willis points to the property grounds' size printed in the corner of the blueprint and asks.

"It's true. When the state hospital was finished, the grounds were that size. As you can see, some buildings were on the other side of the street at one time, but now you wouldn't even know without these blueprints or old stories; it's just empty fields," Paul said, pointing out different places no longer around.

"The state hospital. Do you think there's a way we could get a copy of this blueprint somehow?" Willis asks.

"The only place I can think of for printing these plans would be to take them to the planning and zoning offices; they have a large printer that I have used in the past.

"Before I forget to bring this up, Willis found a name I hadn't heard before while looking at some old microfilms at the library. Have you ever heard before of the name Issac Bernard?" Ted asks Paul.

"That name doesn't ring a bell." Paul replies.

"Isaac Bernard helped start the Vulcan furnace plant in the early days of Newberry." Willis shares.

"The early days of Newberry are a popular time period with plenty of documentation, and I've never seen anything in the museum mention him." Paul shares.

"Maybe that microfilm is the only proof left of Isaac Bernard," Willis replies.

"Boy, these woods have some mighty trees around Newberry. Some trees in these woods could rival anywhere. The Tahquamenon River used to see these massive trees flow down the river daily, pouring truckloads of money into this village."

"You know, Paul, since we made you come all this way and open us to this marvelous place, we should stick around a while longer. This museum has so much good stuff left for us to see. We shouldn't hurry out of here. Could you please entertain an old Marine's love for history and let us stick around for a bit?" Ted asks, looking at an old image in his hands.

"Absolutely," Paul replies.

Ted and Paul walk around the museum, with Ted asking questions challenging Paul's historical knowledge of the area. While waiting for Ted, Willis looks around and discovers a black-and-white picture of a ribbon cutting ceremony on the front steps of his building, the Newberry Building.

"Was this an image of the opening of the Newberry Building?" Willis asks Paul as he holds the picture in Paul's direction.

"Yes, that photo was when the Porters owned the Newberry Building for a short time. The Porters ended up drinking away most of the profits I've heard and losing the place to a foreclosure from the bank, so they didn't own it for long. I heard around town that Thomas Porter wanted it back in the family and planned to buy it before you outbid him for it, Willis. Boy, from the stories I heard around town, Porter was hot over not getting the place; he usually gets whatever he wants around here."

Willis replied, "I've never met Thomas Porter in person, but I've read and heard a lot about him from others. Now it makes more sense why he's never him in my bakery."

"It's best to stay on the good side if you can, but I guess you didn't even get a chance. That man sure can hold grudges; it's a family trait," Paul shares.

CHAPTER 21

As the winter snow quickly melts away from Lake Superior's shoreline, Joy and Archer take a trip up to the shore for rock hunting on a sunny afternoon. While looking at some colorful rocks Archer found, Willis hears the ping of his phone. Willis reached into his hoodie and pulled out his phone. Surprised he had any signal this far north, he looked at the screen and saw a text from Marla, the owner of the Exclusive Moose Gift Store, which is right across the road from Northern Bites. The text states that an individual is pacing back and forth on the rooftop of the Newberry Building, causing concern that they may attempt to jump.

"Somebody's on the rooftop of our building," Willis tells Joy as she puts rocks in a bucket from the shoreline after reading the text.

"Are you kidding me? How did someone get up there?" Joy asks, picking Archer up and starting to head back to their SUV with Willis.

"No idea; Eric also said in the text that the state police are on their way. It seemed like people were gathering outside Northern Bites, around the building. The Newberry Fire Department and EMS had arrived and were trying to contact whoever was on the roof. Let's head back, and I'll take you both over to your parents' house until things calm down," Willis said, helping gather up their belongings and rushing back to Newberry from Lake Superior.

In a rush, Willis drove to the Newberry Building after dropping off Joy and Archer, hoping to prevent any harm to the person on the roof or his property. Willis sees up ahead the lights of the EMS ambulance and a Newberry fire truck blocking Newberry Avenue, the main street in front of his building. Willis drove right behind the emergency vehicles and got out of his SUV. He instantly heard and saw someone from the fire department using a loudspeaker to try to contact the person on the roof. An officer from the state police walks towards Willis, telling him to move his vehicle and that he can't park in the middle of the road. Willis explains that he's the owner of the building.

"We've been trying to reach you for over an hour," the officer says.

"I just received the text thirty minutes ago while at Lake Superior with my family. Did someone break in?" Willis asks.

"The fire department sent a couple of guys over; let's ask the fire chief," the paramedic says, leading Willis towards the fire truck through the crowd.

"Bill, meet Willis Davis. He owns the Newberry Building," the paramedic said, introducing Willis to the fire chief.

"I wish we were meeting under better circumstances for the first time. There seem to be no signs of a break-in on the main floor or the basement entry of your building. Some of my guys walked by all the entrances and exits, and everything was locked. Whoever it is either climbed the escape ladders or found another way up. We're trying to get the person to say something, but no luck so far. No one has a clue who it is up on your roof," Bill shares.

Willis stands quietly in shock as he looks up towards his rooftop, not seeing anyone but knowing someone was on top of his building.

"We've done about everything I can think of, but whoever it is up there is so far back that we can't make out who it is As the tallest building downtown, we can't get a clear view. The only thing we've seen is someone wearing a black hoodie. We tried to go up some other buildings across the street to look, but that didn't help. We're waiting for the state police to arrive before doing anything else. Because there are so many people around, we're being cautious. Who knows if whoever is up there is armed and dangerous?"

Willis continues looking up towards the rooftop as the sun starts to set behind the building, watching to see if he could make out who it was. However, he only sees one individual's shoulder at times for a second.

"Can I try to speak with whoever it is?" Willis asks Bill.

"Worth a shot. Here's the megaphone, but try to keep it brief. I don't want whoever is up there to do something drastic. The last thing this town needs is to see a body flying off the top of your building or bullets flying around," the fire chief says, handing Willis the speaker.

"This is Willis Davis, the owner of the building. We want to help you get down safely." Willis shouts into the blue megaphone.

Willis stood on the rooftop, waiting for a response. Silence filled the air. Suddenly, a loud scream pierced through the stillness. It was a man's voice. Following a moment of silence, a second scream could be heard, along with someone crying. Finally, the man's anguished voice broke the silence. He uttered, "I couldn't even see her again."

Willis instantly recognized Noah's voice as the man on his roof.

"I know that voice. It's Noah," Willis says, still holding the megaphone to the fire chief standing next to him.

"Noah, this is Willis. I recognized your voice. I want to help. Being on my roof is not the right way to handle this. Please come down. I will explain everything to the police when they arrive and won't press any charges, I promise you," Willis says through the megaphone.

"Explain what? Explain how this town turns against its own, calling you a killer. I'm not about to jump from here; I'm just trying to clear my head. The people in this town are the crazy ones. They've been spreading lies about me, putting their noses in everyone else's business. I used to love this town, but now I hate it. I hate all of you. You hear me? Sarah means everything to me. I love her, and I would never hurt her. Shame on you for thinking that I could. You wear a fake smile, but behind my back, you call me a murderer. How could any of you think I killed Sarah? I love her and Ava with everything in my soul, and you've taken that away from me." Noah responds, his voice hoarse from yelling.

'I'm about to come up to you on the roof. Is that okay?" Willis asks Noah, with the fire chief shaking his head in disapproval at the words coming out of Willis's mouth.

"I know you didn't do what some believe you did. I believe you're innocent, and so do others; you're not alone," Willis says into the megaphone.

While Willis and the fire department wait for Noah to come down, the state police department arrives. Willis looks on as Noah climbs down the broken emergency escape railing, grabs onto a window seal, and then some bricks, making his way down the brick walls of the Newberry Building till Noah reaches the ground. Willis walked over to Noah, wiping his hands off from the climb down.

"Thanks for coming down. I was worried about you, Noah," Willis says, standing next to Noah.

"Sorry for going up on your roof like that, Willis; that's where I've cleared my head for years before you bought this place while it sat vacant, but no one noticed me before. Can you take me home?" Noah asks Willis.

"I will, but the state police department will want to speak to you first. The officer seems ticked off, so take it down a notch. When your done speaking to the police, I'll be waiting in my SUV. You just were cleared of having anything to do with the murders, so let's stay out of trouble," Willis says, patting Noah on the back as he starts to walk over to speak with the officer.

Willis observed Noah speaking to the officer. Afterwards, Noah approached Willis's SUV in the rain. He opened the passenger door and sat down, shaking and remaining silent.

"I'm sorry, Noah, that it's come to this. People can be idiots. No one's seen you in weeks. What have you been doing?" Willis asks.

"I just wanted some alone time to escape from my dumb mistakes. Willis, you're one of the few people I really trust. It should've been me instead of Sarah. I love Sarah and Ava more than anything." Noah shared, with tears streaming down his face as he watched the rain.

"I know you do, Noah," Willis replies, driving in the rain.

"How is Ava doing? I miss her so much." Wiping away tears, Noah asks.

"She's doing the best she can. Chelsea and her family are giving her so much love, but I know she misses you. I have some images Ava drew you that Chelsea gave me to bring over to you. Chelsea's family is doing all they can for Ava," Willis says as he reaches into his center console, grabs the art, and hands it to Noah.

"Thank you," Noah says, smiling, looking at Ava's drawings.

"If you ever need a place to go, you know I have plenty of rooms in that big building of mine. Come stay with us if you need a break from your house," Willis says.

"I appreciate the invitation, but for me, my home holds the most meaningful moments with Sarah and Ava. A couple of days after hearing the news, I couldn't leave my bedroom. I kept looking over and closing my eyes, picturing Sarah next to me. Her being gone didn't feel real as long as I stayed home. I might take you up on that offer someday, but right now, I need to watch over my house. Someone's been trespassing on my property. The other day, when I went outside for some fresh air for a minute, when I came back in, I noticed someone had been tampering with my property, and they didn't even bother to hide it. They left my gate open as proof. I need to figure out who has been tampering with my house because I saw footprints in the mud," Noah answers.

Willis and Noah sat in silence in the SUV for a few minutes as they drove to Noah's house.

"I used to believe in God. I did before this mess, but now I just don't know any more. How could a god create such a beautiful world and just sit back and watch all this evil happen before him? All this violence, all the death, and hate? This world is too cruel, and it makes me feel like God left us behind," Noah says, breaking the silence and rubbing his eyes in exhaustion.

"I don't have an honest answer to that, Noah. I'm not a biblical scholar by any means, but I believe we all choose between good and evil every minute of every day. I don't have an excellent answer to why God can stand by and let us destroy one another like we do, but I don't blame Him. We will find out who did this to Sarah and the others. I promise you I will do everything I can to help bring justice for them," Willis tells Noah.

"I bet someone in one of these houses we are driving by knows what happened to Sarah. Maybe we should just walk house to house and get answers. People are just moving on, like every time something horrible happens around here, they're scared to find out what's really happening. This village just doesn't share its secrets; if they would just rat out who's doing this, maybe things would change for the better for us all. Even with my name cleared, I'll never get a second chance in Newberry. Whatever it takes, I'm determined to find out who did this, even if it kills me," Noah says to Willis with a serious look.

Willis reaches Noah's gravel road and turns into his driveway. Before Willis's SUV comes to a complete stop, Noah opens the door, jumping out with his hands in the air in the rain, in disbelief, seeing something that bothers him.

"Look at this crap, Willis. Do you see those footprints right there? Despite all the warning signs and my pit bull, it doesn't scare off whoever it is. Whoever this is messing with me is poking a bear; I've had it," Noah shouts, in frustration, standing in the rain next to Willis's SUV.

"We should call the state police," Willis replies.

"They won't do anything. The police are probably part of this whole mess up here. This drives me crazy that even though I live in America, I can't reach out to anyone within an hour's distance to help end this. It's like the Wild West now; you have to be the law yourself." Noah says, looking around his property for more evidence of trespassers.

"Before you do anything crazy, call me and let's talk through it. If you need help, I will be right over," Willis says as Noah touches the tracks in the mud in his driveway.

"Okay," Noah says in a somber voice, taking off the beanie he always wears and throwing it in the mud as he stands up, running his hands through his hair as he contemplates what to do.

"I mean it, Noah, call me, and I'll be right over. You're not alone in this," Willis says, getting back in his SUV.

As Noah stands in the pouring rain, surveying his surroundings, Willis rolls down his passenger window and gives Noah one last shout before taking off "Take some pictures of these footprints and tracks before they wash away, Noah. You never know how this might come in handy later if you need evidence to get whoever this is. We can send it over to the state police tomorrow," Willis says loudly as the rain gets even stronger.

"That's a good idea. My phone still has some life left to take more pictures around the property," Noah says, looking at his phone's battery life.

"I don't want to leave you if you're not okay. You have just drawn attention from half of downtown by scaling the roof of my building. Are you all right? I can stay for a while." Willis asks.

"I'll be okay. Yelling from the rooftops can soothe your soul. Count me in for dinner tomorrow. I'm going to take a few pictures and call it a night. I haven't slept well in days, so I need to crash. Thanks for not thinking I'm crazy, Willis," Noah says while taking some photos in the pouring rain.

"You still have so much to give, Ava and the world, and you are a good father. She will return to you quickly. Do not forget to charge that phone. I will call to check in on you later," Willis says as he waves goodbye, drives off, and looks in his rearview mirror to see Noah taking more pictures in the rain.

CHAPTER 22

With Chelsea's help, Willis set up a meeting with Joe Benjamin at the Chippewa reservation just outside Newberry to discuss some new information on Sarah's death. The reservation seems distant from the town, but it is located just outside the village boundaries and is home to some of the most beautiful recently constructed houses in the area. Willis drove slowly through the reservation. In the distance, he noticed two boys around his son's age. They had stopped playing on a swing set and were staring at him as he passed by. As Willis drove past, the boys who were staring at him smiled and waved. Willis's car navigation system alerted him, saying, Your destination is on the left.

Joe wheeled himself to the door and opened it for Willis.

"Come on in, sorry for the mess; I don't get many visitors," Joe shares.

Willis entered the house and surveyed the surroundings. It was a small and cluttered space, filled with books and magazines piled on every surface. The air carried a faint aroma of cooking.

"Thanks for letting me come over. I've never been to the reservation before; it always felt like a place I needed to be invited to. My son would love the playground," Willis says, settling down beside Joe.

"Bring your son over any time to play; the children around the reservation would love to have him as a guest. The reservation has been a blessing for our families. My grandparents lived in the old Native American area of the village. My grandparents' generation grew up in cramped shacks without running water or bathrooms. We have made significant progress since then. However, everyone does not accept my people outside of the reservation." Joes replies.

"You deserve what you have here and so much more. Thanks for all you've done and all the posters over the years for all those that have gone missing. Chelsea mentioned you had a few things you wanted to show me," Willis says.

"I do. I wanted to give Chelsea what I've found to show you, but I thought it would be best to show you here on the reservation. After my car accident, I had to find something to do with myself after my hockey dreams ended. I wanted to make something of myself and knew leaving here was probably off the cards. The reservation is a safe haven and a very close community; Sarah was one of us, like a sister to me. From what Chelsea shared with me, you've been looking into the family lines around here. I have something you may not have seen," Joe says as he wheels himself over to his computer desk in his wheelchair. Looking around his desk with papers scattered everywhere, he grabs a small leather notebook underneath some other books and hands it over to Willis.

Willis pulls off the leather strap on the notebook and opens it.

"This journal belonged to Sarah's great-grandmother, Elu. Sarah recently received the journal from her grandmother, Enola. You might recognize a name or two, so feel free to look at it," says Joe. Willis opens the journal pages, reading through what seems like love letters between Sarah's great-grandmother Elu and someone, and then sees the man's name.

To my deepest love, Isaac Bernard.

"Isaac Bernard? Isaac was married."

"You'll want to keep reading," Joe says, looking up at Willis as he continues to read the journal.

Willis is looking through Elu's journal. He finds a sealed letter placed inside the pages. Isaac sent the letter back to Elu, Sarah's grandmother. Someone stapled the letter to a page.

"At some point before Isaac Bernard's family came up to live in Newberry with him, Isaac met Elu and fell in love with her. Sarah's great-grandmother Elu never married, but she had a daughter named Enola, who was Isaac's child. During those days, relationships between our people and the white man weren't allowed and were even illegal for multiple years. During the bubonic plague in 1922, Isaac's wife and children all died, leaving Enola, Sarah's grandmother, as a young child to inherit all the money and land Isaac earned from managing the Vulcan Furnace in Newberry. The Hughes and Porter families claimed the land without the legal right to do so, believing that Enola's claim to the inheritance would never hold up in court. However, times have changed, and the courts might look at it differently. To me, it all happened to Sarah because of that journal, and somehow those families found out about it. I have a stack of letters between Elu and Isaac talking about Enola as his child. These letters and the journal are probably the only proof that the land belongs to Sarah. It's just a theory, but I believe Sarah's strong-willed personality and her willingness to confront the Porters likely caused significant problems between her and the Porter family."

"I wish I could've known Sarah; she seems like such a brave, courageous woman," Willis responds, looking at an old picture of Sarah as a child with her great grandmother Enola.

"One other thing I noticed looking over the reports of the recent missing people is that after they find the bodies, the locations seem to be connected. Joe reaches over and pulls out a piece of paper. He had hand-drawn the locations of all those who had gone missing recently.

"The individual locations may appear random, but when combined, they reveal a strong connection. The bodies have all been found near the Dollarville Dam or by Lake Superior, within a few miles of each disappearance on state land. So that tribal police can't investigate it because the bodies are located outside the reservation. Whoever is doing this is the same person with the same habits."

"Can I take a picture of this sketch with my phone?" Willis asks.

"Yes, of course, you may keep this paper. After going through several edits, I hope that this is the last time I add someone missing to the list. One other thing that's promising to find out what's truly going on and whose behind it is a lead came in a few days ago. Chelsea's mother brought over some mail she had opened about Sarah's making sure all her bills were taken care of. I noticed a significant deposit in her bank statement. On the statement, you can see Sarah sent a return wire back to the account," Joe says, pointing to a wire transfer transaction of $300,000 Sarah sent back.

"Who sent the wire to Sarah?" Willis asks.

"No one knows. That's what I'm trying to find out. I thought, with your background in investigating, you might have some ideas of how to get this information. You're the best chance we have of finding who did this transfer and who killed Sarah."

"The bank should have all the account information and a record of it. Everything has a paper trail." Willis replies, looking at the transactions.

"The problem is that, since the rest of Sarah's family has passed away, only four-year-old Ava has the legal right to view it. Chelsea and others on the reservation are trying to find a legal way to access Sarah's accounts," Joe replied.

After reading the statement, Willis makes a note of the bank's name and phone number in case he comes up with a solution. "Over the last couple of years, we've had multiple members of our tribe vanish without a trace when they left the reservation. The tribal police haven't given up on finding them, but without the state police helping, there's only so far they can go outside their jurisdiction. Also, please don't mention you stopped by the reservation to anyone or my name. I'm safe on the reservation; no one would be foolish enough to come in here, but you're out in the open, so I would watch your back. The number of killings and missing people seems to be escalating recently," Joe says, wheeling himself over to his living room window and looking out.

Willis follows Joe over to the window, seeing Ava playing outside next door in the front yard of Chelsea's mother's house, jumping and smiling while chasing after soap bubbles Chelsea's mother blows in the wind in Ava's direction.

"I fight for truth for people like Ava," Joe says, looking up at Willis from his wheelchair. "So that her generation can have a better life than we do, just like my ancestors fought for me."

As Willis leaves the reservation, he sees a truck. He glances in his rear-view mirror and sees the truck following him in the distance. Willis tries to see who's driving, but it's too far away. He slows down as he enters town and pulls into the Holiday gas station, pretending to pump gas while he watches for the truck to pass. However, the truck never shows up.

CHAPTER 23

In the Upper Peninsula, springtime arrives swiftly, and the last of the snowmelts quickly. On a bright, cloudless weekend morning, Willis takes Archer out fishing for the first time at the Dollarville Dam. The Dollarville Dam is a hidden paradise for anglers, secluded behind train tracks, marsh land, and tall lumber piles. While buying fishing gear at the local sports shop, Duke's Sports Shop, the owner, Eddie, said the dam's waters harness some of the most outstanding trout fishing in all of Michigan. The quiet remoteness and sounds of the rushing waters have made the dam one of Willis's favorite spots to escape from the daily grind of work life to escape and enjoy the evening sunsets. The walk to the dam from the parking lot is a long dirt trail with ponds on both sides filled with beautiful tall grass springing to life with early spring wildflowers. As they make their way to the dam, Archer reaches down to pluck some wildflowers to give his mother as a gift.

When Willis was younger, he went fishing in Missouri a couple of times with his mother. However, he caught his shoe more than a fish, as his mother liked to remind him. Willis and Archer found that catching fish was more challenging than Willis expected. It took them some trial-and-error to learn the best techniques. Duke's Sports Shop guaranteed the bait Willis purchased was the right bait for attracting fish at the dam. Willis looked back toward the trail and saw his friend Kevin walking his way with fishing gear. Kevin was a giant of a man, standing over six and a half feet tall and built like a football lineman. In a matter of weeks, Kevin and Willis became close friends because of Kevin's witty humor and love for Kevin Smith films.

"It's great to see you out here fishing with young Archer. Have you ever fished before?" Kevin asked.

"Not in decades. I bet all my brand-new gear gives it away." Willis jokingly replies while having issues fixing a fishing lure.

"I think what gave it away was the price tags still on your tackle box and fishing rod. My friend, it is better to learn by watching someone who knows how to attach the lure than to mess it all up. Let me show you."

After spending some time learning how to fish the waters of the Dollarville Dam from Kevin, after a successful fishing trip, Kevin packed up for the day, having caught the perch he had hoped to catch.

"Enjoy this time with your son because it goes by too quickly. I will visit Northern Bites early in the morning to learn about your catches," Kevin says as he reaches over, picking up his tackle box and cooler, and walking away with his rod over his shoulder.

After catching a few small fish and enjoying the time with Archer, Willis took a couple more casts of his fishing pole, but this time he badly tangled his line.

"Look, Dad, I see a fish; it's huge," Archer says, pointing to the water as a large perch floats by right in front of them, close enough to shore that they could almost pick it up.

Willis rushes to fix the line, knowing he might not get a chance like this again. Struggling with the fishing line and the fish moving downstream, Willis notices someone walking down the trail in his direction. As Willis continued to try to fix his line by himself, kneeling and focusing intently, he heard the man set down his tackle box next to him.

"It looks like you have a mess there. How about you let me help you out, boy?" the man says behind Willis.

Willis immediately recognized the unique, raspy baritone voice as soon as he heard it. He had heard so much about this voice, and he knew it belonged to none other than Thomas Porter.

"Appreciate the help," Willis responds, standing back up and wondering if this moment was a random encounter or on purpose.

"Boy, you have made quite a mess here." Thomas Porter says, straightening out the tackle on the fishing line and inspecting Willis's fishing pole.

Willis is confused about whether he is alluding to the line or the events he is looking into in the village.

"So, you're the Kansas City kid? Willis, right? You're the one that outbid me on the Newberry Building; well done. My grandpa made a mess of that place, but I had some big plans for that building. I have heard so much about you; you are very well-liked in this town for what you have done with the building," Thomas shares while fixing the fishing line.

"That's me. I hope there are no hard feelings about us owning the Newberry Building. I appreciate the help on the fishing line. My son and I were about to call it a day. We weren't having much luck out here," Willis says, starting to put things away in his tackle box quickly.

"Come on, stick around. You don't want to leave now, do you? Look at all the perch just waiting for your boy to catch them," Thomas says, casting out Willis's fishing pole line.

Willis watches on nervously, keeping Archer close to his side.

"It's a balance between the river and the fish. Do you see it?" Thomas asks, looking over at Archer.

"I don't see anything," Archer says, walking closer, looking intently in at the rushing water.

"See, the river on this side of the dam guides the fish over it. They need this guidance; otherwise, all the fish will starve or never leave the pond. They need the river to lead them," Thomas says, looking over at Willis, with Archer standing by and watching the fishing line get tight from the perch going for the bait.

"The fish could all perish if one of them veers off course and takes the others with it. You want to reel in that big fish, son?" Thomas Porter asks Archer with a smile, then stares up at Willis with a serious face.

"Absolutely," Archer replied with enthusiasm, eagerly clutching the fishing rod while Thomas Porter gradually reeled in the line, all while Archer watched intently.

"Notice how the fishing line tightened? This indicates that he is where you want him to be and that you are in control of the fish's life. When you catch a fish, son, you have two options. Do you kill the fish or release it back into the water? What decision would you make?"

"I would let it go," Archer replies.

"You're sure, even if it's a bad fish?" Thomas asks, looking over at Willis.

"Yep," Archer said, looking at the perch as it came out of the water, fighting to break free from the line.

"But what if this one takes all the other fish in the wrong direction and they do not follow the river?" Says Thomas, meeting Willis's gaze as he hoists the fish into the air, where it battles for freedom against the fishing line.

"The fish won't; he's a good fish," Archer says, smiling as the fish dangled wildly in the air in front of him.

"I'll trust your judgment, young friend. I hope you're right," Thomas says as he removes the fish from the hook and places it back in the rushing water below.

Willis reached down and grabbed his tackle box with one hand. He picked up Archer with his other hand as the boy stared at the water, waiting to see the fish swim away. "Time to go, Archer," Willis said.

"Dad, look! The fish is sleeping on top of the water," Archer says to Willis, looking over his shoulder and pointing at the fish Thomas just put back in the river, now floating dead downstream.

"Sometimes they never adjust back in the water, as they should, and don't make it. I'll let you explain that part to your boy." As Thomas Porter handed Willis back his fishing pole, Archer watched the perch float lifelessly further downstream.

Thomas Porter walks away facing the other side of the dam and says, "Fishing's better on this side. See you around town." He whistled as he threw his fishing line into the water.

Willis walked away in silence. He carried his son and fishing gear in his arms as he made his way back up the trail to his SUV. During the walk back, he pondered what had just occurred. He realized he had crossed a line that was irreversible.

CHAPTER 24

Willis has a lot to tell Larry about the Porters, including his meeting with Thomas Porter at the dam and the information he learned about Sarah from visiting Joe on the reservation. The perfect time to discuss the latest developments after months of conversations at Northern Bites over who's behind all these problems in Newberry has arrived. Willis is invited to see Larry's completed labyrinth creation in person at his home. Willis had driven down many back roads in the Newberry area, but he had never experienced the country roads outside of McMillan, a small town next to Newberry. The gravel road to Larry's reminds Willis of his childhood car rides in the countryside back in Missouri. Willis drove with his windows down, the wind whipping through his hair as he passed by small ponds and fields on a straight, flat gravel road that stretched out before him as far as the eye could see. The road was so straight, you could have driven it with your eyes closed. The long, winding road was flanked by whispering trees. As the road comes to an end, it splits into two routes. The road splits into two directions: to the left is a boat launch that leads into East Lake; to the right is a residence that can be accessed through a sizable metal gate. Willis turned right and drove through the metal gate between the two stone pillars. Lilac bushes were in full bloom, filling the air with their sweet scent. As he drove down the driveway, Willis admired the beautiful art pieces and neatly stacked wood piles surrounding him.

Up ahead, Willis can see Larry's farmhouse, a large blue Victorian-style home in the middle of an open field. As Willis pulls up to the house, Larry walks out the front door and down his front steps towards Willis's SUV to greet him.

"Glad you made it, Willis. Today is a perfect day to see my labyrinth with no clouds in the sky. Daylight is quickly fading, so let's head to my backyard. I hope you're up for a challenge. I want to see how fast you can make it through," Larry says.

Larry led Willis around the corner of the house, revealing the tall green labyrinth opening with the sun shining directly behind it. The entrance to the labyrinth felt like it had popped off the pages of a book, with emerald-green bushes rising high above a backyard fence that bent in the distance.

"Give it a shot. Let's see if you can get through without anyone's help. I have only shown the labyrinth to three people before you. The best time through the labyrinth so far is thirty-five minutes. Starting my timer now, let's see how you do," Larry says, pulling out a stopwatch from his pocket and clicking it.

"Are you serious? I just got here," Willis responds.

"Time's ticking," Larry says, looking at Willis holding his stopwatch.

Willis has to decide quickly whether to go left or right as he dashes over to the labyrinth's entrance. With every turn in the maze, Willis tries to keep his composure, remembering his past turns to not make the same mistake twice, but everything looks so similar that it all becomes a blur quickly. After just minutes, Willis feels more confused. Rather than overthinking it, Willis decides he won't worry about how far he's made it through, and just follow his instinct. Minutes later, Willis makes it through to the exit, which is a large opening, with Larry standing next to the exit, staring at his stopwatch. Willis raced past Larry and stopped to catch his breath. He turned to look behind Larry and noticed the massive stone pillars arranged in a Stonehenge-like pattern. The sun was setting, and its rays shone through the center of the stone structure.

"Do you want to know your time?" Larry asked with a look of disappointment on his face.

My time must be terrible based on the expression on your face. I am really out of shape from sitting around all winter," Willis replies, remaining hunched over and gasping for air.

"Actually, you set a record time, beating even my personal best time. Seventeen minutes and forty-one seconds. Impressive," Larry says, showing Willis his time.

"Your best time? Didn't you build this thing?" Willis asks.

"Yep, all by myself," Larry replies with a smile.

"So, you're telling me it still takes you that long to complete the labyrinth?" Willis asked, puzzled.

"Since I built this myself and know all the tricks, I only count my attempts to master the labyrinth when I have a substantial amount of homemade moonshine in my blood," Larry replies, laughing.

"I would pay lots of money to see a wasted Larry trying to make it through this labyrinth," Willis responds.

"I made sure that the security camera footage of me running around in my underwear carrying a torch, falling through the labyrinth, and passing out on my front porch would never leave my property. The closest you'll ever get to that footage is hearing the story I just told you."

"Can I bribe you with free coffee?" Willis asks.

"Tempting, but not going to happen; no one's ever getting their hands on that footage. I should delete it. This town already thinks I'm crazy enough," Larry muttered, looking up at the sun before walking over to the center of his homemade Stonehenge. He kneels down, wiping away leaves covering a hand-carved star in the city of stone structure, with the sunlight directly running into it with the leaves gone, creating a brightly lit shooting star on the stone slab.

"Amazing. I have to take a video to show Joy and Archer, or they won't believe it. This is remarkable," Willis says, reaching into his pocket for his phone and taking a quick video with it.

"Put the phone down, Willis, and see it with your own eyes, my friend. This will only last for a few more seconds. The only thing that remotely compares to this is the aurora borealis northern lights off the shores of Lake Superior." Larry remarks as the sun gradually sets behind the shooting star stone.

"Building this must've been a huge undertaking to line it up just right," Willis responds.

"It took a bit of trial and error, but those brilliant ancestors of ours that dragged the stones from Wales over to England did all the hard work and calculations. All I had to do was follow their methods. The toughest part is having the sunlight align perfectly with the stone. I tweaked the way Stonehenge's builders handled the solstice so that I could get the same effect on any clear night. All you have to do is make sure you're on time," Larry responded as he touched one of the stone pillars, reminiscing over making the structure.

Larry shares with Willis his dream of creating his own Woodhenge on his property next to the Newberry State Hospital grounds, using large pieces of lumber to do so. Larry explains that the Newberry Woodhenge location is perfect, with the old barns and silos from the Newberry State Hospital in the background. He believes his father would approve of the idea.

Larry shares with Willis the additional reason for inviting only him to his home rather than the entire family. Larry, knowing that Willis has not given up on discovering what happened to Sarah and the others. Larry tells Willis he has something in his work shed that might be a strong lead to who is involved. As they walk over to the shed, Willis shares his recent visit to the reservation and the shocking details of Sarah being related to Isaac Bernard, the original manager of the Vulcan Furnace company, and Sarah's inheritance.

As Willis enters the large shed, Larry flips on the light switch as they walk in. As the lights slowly flicker on from the fluorescent bulbs, Willis sees stacks of old items that must have come from the Newberry State Hospital grounds after its closing. The items are stacked on shelves on one side of the work shed and, on the other wall, a workbench running from wall to wall.

"You told me a few days ago while chatting at Northern Bites that you and Ted ventured out to the museum and got a copy of the building prints copied from the state hospital, and possibly word got around to some of the locals you were still looking into Sarah's case."

"We did. I even had an unexpected visit from Thomas Porter at the Dollarville Dam while fishing with my son."

"Well, at least to me, that confirms you're heading down the right path, so I wanted to give you this," Larry responds as he reaches up to a shelf, pulling down a big roll of large papers.

"What is it?" Willis asks.

"Let me show you," Larry responds as he removes the rubber bands and opens up the papers on the workbench, bending down a lamp over the documents.

"These prints in front of you are the ones you want; you can discard the others. These final prints were used in 1964 to complete the construction of the grounds

149

surrounding Newberry State Hospital. My father, when he left his office for the last time, took the prints with him. These blueprints show the final layout of the barns next to my property, which show an underground system not shown on any other set I've seen or heard about running all the way to the state hospital main buildings and having extra storage underground. I put up a 'no trespassing' sign and a couple of trail cams after seeing large sets of tire tracks on my property multiple times. I aimed the cameras at the hospital grounds and the lumberyard operated by the Porters to ensure that no one would bother me. So far, all the trail cams have recorded are a couple of teens using my land as a shortcut across the field and two black bears, until last weekend. Look at this," Larry says intently.

Larry turns on a computer monitor on his workbench, guides his computer mouse to open a trail cam footage folder, and clicks on a video file.

"This side of the state hospital grounds by the old barn has remained untouched since the early 1980s. It's one of the first areas to shut down and is so far away from everything else. I would think it would be odd for a security check over this far from the prison, but then this happened." Larry runs the video forward until a prison guard walks the frame, and then he pauses the video.

"Is that a prison guard guarding the barn entrance with a flashlight?" Observing the paused video clip, Willis poses the question.

Larry presses play on the video again, showing the front of a truck pulling into view with its headlights shining on the barn door, and then the truck lights shut off.

"I've seen that truck around town. That's the same truck that followed me around when I left the reservation a few days ago," Willis responds, noticing the truck.

"The video shows more events, and that truck is coming from Porter's lumberyard," Larry remarks as it plays.

Willis and Larry watch on as the video shows the flashlight of the correctional officer facing the barn as two other people follow him into the barn, and the prison guard comes back outside to stand by its entrance.

""The video was recorded at 3 a.m., and within the next twenty minutes, it caught the guard carefully watching two people coming in and out with something. Once they leave the barn, nothing else really happens except for the prison guard locking the door and heading back to the state hospital. I really need a better trail camera. The barn footage is too blurry to make out who went in," Larry said, pausing the video.

"Whatever is going on in that barn can't be good. Maybe we can find out who was on duty for patrol that night at the prison," Willis says.

"I have seen this several times, and if anyone could hide a drug hideout or these killings from the village's residents and the state police, it would have to be someone who feels like they have total control over everyone and everything. To you, who does that sound like?" Larry asks Willis after turning off the video clip

"I can't think of a single reason someone would be out that late doing anything legal or daring enough to mess around on state-owned prison land except for Thomas Porter," Willis responds.

"That man thinks he's a god around here. I moved my cameras closer to get a better look at the truck and the people if they come back again."

"Maybe we should show this video clip to the prison warden or the state police," Willis replies.

"Ha, I believe the warden is involved in the situation at the barn. We don't know how deep this reaches or who's involved. I only trust you with this evidence, Willis; with proof like this, I cannot trust anyone in this town, not even my barber or the prison warden. I don't think there's enough evidence here yet to mean anything. All we have is some guys opening up a vacant old barn door, and we can't even identify them. Who knows, I could be making this all up in my head. I wanted to show you this footage just in case something happens to me." With concern in his voice, Larry states this.

"Do you think they would try to kill you or me over this?" Willis asks.

"If the Porters are involved, I would not rule it out. The Porters could have recently killed three people in a burning car. I made you a flash drive to bring home the footage I have so far from my trail camera," Larry says, handing Willis the flash drive.

"Maybe we should find someone we can trust to give this footage, along with everything else we have so far. What if we email or call the attorney general's office?" Willis asks.

"The attorney general would do nothing with it. We need hard evidence that locks them up forever, or the Porters will come right after us."

"I have my family to watch out for. How about I tell Bob about this and show him? He would make sure it got to the right people, or he would investigate it," Willis asks.

"I know you trust Bob, and so do I. Bob's an honest man, but someone like him at his age could become the next victim before he could do anything with it, and then it would come straight back to us. One wrong move or conversation, and everything we've done so far is over," Larry says.

"Something just hit me. Let's look at those prints one more time. Look right here. Someone used this underground area in the barn for storage, and it runs through the entire building. The Porters could store anything they wanted in that place, and it would be out of sight," Willis remarks, examining the blueprints.

"Who in their right mind would store drugs or missing people right on the edges of the prison grounds when you live in one of the remotest places in the country?" Larry asks, walking around the room.

"Someone who isn't afraid of anything, who thinks he controls everything, including the prison itself, has a god complex. The more pressing question is what's going on in there. We can make all the assumptions in the world, but we just don't know. Do you think one of us could sneak over during the day somehow into the barn unnoticed?" Willis asks.

"It's way too dangerous to go during daylight or at night; we will have to find out what's inside another way. One wrong step, and they could move whatever is happening in that old barn to somewhere we will never find. Right now, the Porters have no clue what we know, and that's how we must keep it. We will only have one shot, no matter the plan we put together. With you having a family, I didn't want you to get to much more involved. I would go into the barn myself, but I can guarantee Porter has people watching me all around town since we're neighbors now. It will be tricky to figure out what's in that barn. Make sure you don't tell your father-in-law or wife about it. It's for their safety. I want you to take these plans with you," Larry says as he hands the plans to Willis, and they walk out of the shed.

Willis puts the plans in his trunk and heads to pick up Joy and Archer from Ted's house. When Willis arrives, he carries in the Newberry State Hospital plans Larry gave him. He says nothing about the trail camera footage or his

153

recent run-in with Thomas Porter while fishing, even though it hurts to hide what he knows from those he loves.

"How was Larry's maze, and what do you have in your hands?" Ted asked, putting down a puzzle piece and taking off his glasses as Willis walks in.

"The labyrinth was incredible. It's hard to put into words just how remarkable it is. Someday soon, it would be great to bring you all over to see it for yourself. This is the last set of prints ever made of the Newberry State Hospital. Larry's father took the final set with him as a parting gift, and Larry gave them to me, though I still plan to give the plans back after I show you." Willis shares.

"This puzzle can wait; let's take a look at that piece of local priceless history in your hands. I was about to drive myself mad any way trying to find where this piece in my hand went," Ted says, getting Willis's help, moving the puzzle from the kitchen table, and laying out the blueprints.

"These prints are priceless. They bring back so many fond memories. You can see that they never built some of these places before the state hospital closed down. Look at those other massive barns they planned to add; they are twice as long as the ones that stand there now," Ted says, pointing at places all over the blueprints.

"If you look over here over to the left, you can see this plan includes the expansion of the underground walkway from the state hospital buildings to the barn area. What memories do you have of the old barns?" Willis asks Ted.

"Very little. It's been ages; you must remember, Willis, when I ran around those grounds while my mother worked in the theater building. Livestock filled the barns. I only went inside to bring back extra milk from the cattle. I remember the size of the interior from my childhood, sixty years ago. Everything seemed enormous back then."

During their conversation, Willis almost accidentally mentions the barn footage he saw at Larry's house but immediately stops himself. The phone rings as Willis and Ted sit in the living room, and Ruth picks it up, looking concerned. Willis hears Ruth say, "Oh no," to whoever was on the other end, piquing his interest in the call. Ruth turns to face him across the living room. Ted continued to talk about old memories of the hospital grounds, but Willis's attention was on Ruth's call. She hung up the phone and walked into the living room, stopping and looking scared to share what she was about to say.

"Noah's dead," Ruth said, her voice breaking. with tears dropping from her eyes, looking towards Willis and Ted. "They found Noah in the woods, out towards Deer Park, just off the cliffs of Lake Superior. I'm so sorry."

"Not Noah. When will all this end?" Joy's says with her voice barely audible as she whispers, her trembling hands pressed together. Willis, in shock himself, walked over and silently stood by her side, offering comfort. With Noah's unexpected death, the room was overcome with the weight of the moment's uncertainty and gravity.

CHAPTER 25

The next day after Noah's death, Willis opened Northern Bites, as usual. The word of Noah's passing spread fast throughout Newberry, as patrons shared their memories of him all morning. As Willis wraps up the morning rush, he notices Justin at the end of the line—the owner of a local sled dog kennel who has grown to be a close friend.

"I'm glad to see you, Justin. It's been a rough morning with the news of Noah's death." Willis shares with Justin while finishing up a drink order.

"I'm the one who found Noah," Justin simply replies in a somber voice.

With his full train of thought lost in what Justin said, Willis stops making the order.

"How did you find Noah?" Willis asks.

"I took my sled dogs out for a late afternoon run by Lake Superior, close to your father-in-law's property near Deer Park, and saw something in the distance laying against a tree. I took my dogs over to see what it was that looked out of place, and it was Noah leaning against a good-sized spruce tree, looking like he was sleeping with no coat on. I've never seen a dead body before and hope I never have to again. After the shock wore off, I didn't know what to do, as I couldn't make a call that far north. After taking a picture of Noah there, I rode my sled as quickly as I could back the two miles or so it would take me to get to someone I knew would be at home. I called 911, and then I went back to be next to Noah until someone could arrive to take him out of the woods. Who knows what would've happened to Noah's body if he were left alone with all the wildlife around? I waited next to Noah for hours until the state police and the EMTs arrived to take care of his body."

"Thanks for staying with Noah. I know that had to be hard. Any sign of how he got there?" Willis asks.

"Hard to say, but he was all alone. While I waited, I took photos of the surroundings and Noah in case something happened. The state police never found his truck or any signs of how he got to the woods while I was there," Justin shares.

"I just can't understand why Noah would be up by Lake Superior. I took him home after the incident on my roof a couple of days ago and texted him to make sure he was okay. Noah responded that he was doing well. Someone must have taken him out there."

"As I stood next to Noah, waiting for the state police, I kept asking myself how he got there—deep in the woods, against a tree—but nothing made sense. There is nothing for miles around that spot by Lake Superior, which is in one of the most isolated areas of this region If foul play was involved, maybe they left him out there, thinking no one would ever find him. "Wouldn't you just throw the body into Lake Superior? It hurts to say this out loud," Justin asks.

"Yes, unless you wanted someone to evidentially find him out there. This might be an odd question, but could I see the photo you took?" Willis asks.

"Sure thing." Justin reaches into his jacket for his phone, bringing up the image of Noah's body laying up against a tree, and hands it to Willis.

"It's heartbreaking," Willis said with a sigh. "It's tough to see him like that. Noah had so much more to give to this world."

"Yes, I saw a bruise on his right arm while waiting for the EMTs to arrive. I did not want to touch him in case there was foul play. You can see in the photo," Justin says, pointing to Noah's right arm.

Willis zooms in on the phone to look at the bruise. "Look, you can see a small needle mark that caused the bruising. One thing I know about Noah is that he is a heavy drinker but not a drug addict. Someone drugged him. Justin, I'll have coverage in about an hour. Are you returning to the kennel or will you still be in town?" Willis asks.

"I'll be in town all day," Justin responds.

"Could you take me to the place in the woods where it happened by chance? Considering how close to his property we are, I might ask Ted if he would like to join us," Willis asks.

"Not a problem. We can take my Jeep out; those roads are really rough right now."

Willis drives over to Ted's mill, letting him know he was heading out by his property to the spot Justin found Noah, if he wanted to come along. Ted shuts down his mill for the day and rides with Willis to meet Justin back at Northern Bites.

As they travel north of Newberry in Justin's Jeep, passing by Oswald's Bear Ranch and Halfway Lake, Ted shares stories of the changes over the years.

Turning into the woods, Justin follows an old camp road that used to be a freight train route. As they drove down the dirt camp roads, Willis pointed out the snow still lingering under the thick pine boughs in the woods.

Ted, sitting in the back seat of the Jeep, shares stories of how in some parts of the woods up north, the snow never fully melts because of the freezing winds from Lake Superior and the shade from the trees. Justin slows down and turns off the Jeep, announcing that they have arrived.

They approached the tree where Noah was found, keeping their distance. Willis takes photos of the area and the tracks. I just shared that the state police questioned him for a few hours, and they tried to contact Noah's family, who live in the Amish community without a telephone. Eventually, neighbors in Engadine informed them of the news. Justin shares that the state police also took photos of the tracks in the vicinity and on the camp road. Willis expresses his belief that whoever killed Noah did so to send a message or as a warning. He looks out at Lake Superior's crashing waves from the cliff's edge. Suddenly, they hear a deep grunt coming from the woods. Ted, Willis, and Justin cautiously look around until they spot a large bull moose. Justin signals for everyone to be quiet. A moose, followed closely by a calf, is approaching. The three hide behind a tree stump and wait for the moose to move away before stepping out.

"Thank goodness we did not startle the mature moose. When those bull moose have their young with them, they can become extremely hostile and dangerous. If there is one thing I do not want to run into in the woods, it is a pissed-off bull moose," Justin quietly says to Ted and Willis as the bull moose moves further away until it is out of sight.

"That moose was massive. I've never seen one in person," Willis says.

"We're in moose territory out here. It's a beautiful but dangerous place," Justin says.

Before heading out, Willis, Ted, and Justin all make their way to the sand-covered camp road, following it up to an opening to view Lake Superior. As the sun sets, a riot of pinks, purples, and blues fills the sky. Ted and Willis watch their reflections shimmer in the endless expanse of Lake Superior.

"Oh, if only these woods could talk, the secrets they could share of things that have happened here and never left. For decades I used to leave my truck running with the windows open all over town, no matter what time of day. It never even crossed my mind to lock the doors. Now I can't do that anymore, and I miss it. I will fight with everything left in this old body to bring that back," Ted says as his voice cuts through the crisp air. As he sternly addresses Willis after looking out over Lake Superior on the edge of the cliff.

Willis had never witnessed Ted speak with such an enraged, despondent, and grave demeanor. The intensity in his voice, the furrowed brows, and the clenched fists conveyed the depth of his emotions. Willis could feel the collective despair that hung in the atmosphere, as if it were a tangible presence. It was undeniable that this relentless cycle of violence needed to end.

CHAPTER 26

Two days later, just as spring had finally arrived, a cold front filled Northern Bites with a morning chill. As Willis was just opening for the day, checking the thermostat, he noticed someone walking back and forth outside the front of Northern Bites through the partially frost-covered windows, blocked by the window frames and walls. All Willis can see is someone's shoulder outside the frosty glass and their breath in the frosty morning air. As Willis walks to the door, he can finally see that it's Neal, the undercover narcotics agent. Willis opens the front door, hearing the sirens from multiple emergency vehicles outside as Neal makes his way into Northern Bites.

"It's all over. We finally got them," Neal says, walking around the bakery with excitement, dressed in his narcotic unit uniform this time instead of coming in wearing a disguise like usual.

Waiting to hear more from Neal regarding the large bust, Willis retreats behind the counter at Northern Bites.

"My task force busted the house minutes ago with all of them in it."

"Who?" Willis asks.

"Mother Mary, she's going away forever this time. The state police will release the names of the others involved to the public soon, but it involves Mother Mary and her family. Mary and the others will not cause pain and attempt to destroy what makes Newberry so special for her or the others on any other day. One of our agents was working undercover, and my unit found so much evidence. To celebrate this being over, I want to buy a round of donuts and some coffee for my guys. It feels good to wrap this bust up successfully after all this time." Neal says, with relief in his voice.

"Now this is how to start a day; that's good news. Whatever you want, your order is on the house! How many do you need?" Willis asks.

"Thanks; I appreciate it. Six coffees and some of those maple donuts should do it. The case had been stalled for weeks, but everything changed a few days ago when we received an anonymous tip that led us to the location and time of the meetup. I can't say much more right now, but this is what we've been waiting for. This is it. This is the thing that will bring everything to an end."

"I never thought this would actually lead to Mary after seeing her in here. She just got out of prison and is so old now Although I had some different theories about who might be responsible for everything, I am glad you were able to stop it. I had my suspicions, but I didn't think she'd be so crazy as to start selling drugs again so soon after getting out of prison and in her old age. I'm glad you were able to put a stop to it. It must be impossible to leave that world once you are in it. When I called you a couple of weeks ago to tell you that she was here with her grandchildren, I was shocked to learn that she was a drug dealer and a murderer. She seemed like such a loving grandmother. I hope the grandchildren weren't at the house during the raid." Willis shares,

"We try to guard the little ones as much as possible, but sometimes it's impossible, like this morning. I believe we counted three children out of the thirteen people in that small house. We pulled the kids out as quickly as possible, just in case things got messy. All the kids are on their way to family services," Neal shares.

"I can't wait to tell Joy that this is all over. All of this has been so hard on us and the community for so long." Willis says, putting maple donuts in a to-go box for Neal.

Awoken by the sirens, Joy walks into Northern Bites as Willis gets ready to help Neal with his drink order outside. "I promise, these sirens are the ones you'll be glad to hear. Neal and his unit just busted Sarah's killer and the drug ring all at once, just down the road. It was Mother Mary and her family." Willis responded.

"Really?" Joy asks.

"Neal just came by to grab some donuts and coffee for the team and share the good news with us."

"Thank you so much, Neal, for risking your life for us and this town. I hope everyone is okay," Joy says.

"There were no injuries; it happened as smoothly as possible. My family lives in town, and this is the first time in a long time that I feel my family will be safe outside around here. We found so much evidence on site that connects those arrested minutes ago to the recent murders and the increase in drug use, and we will lock them away for good. It will take years for anyone to try to do anything evil like this again in Newberry. Well, I better get these coffees over to the guys," Neal says, heading out the door with Willis helping him load the drinks into his truck.

Willis waved goodbye as Neal drove away. He shivered in the cold and headed back inside Northern Bites.

"Did Neal say who it was behind it all?" Joy asks Willis as he walks back in from helping Neal.

"That old lady, Mother Mary, and some others."

"Seriously? That old lady with the cane? She looked harmless; the wind could've taken her out," Joy says.

"Now your dad can keep his truck running while running errands around town," Willis says, holding Joy close.

"I can already see the excitement in my mother's eyes. I have to call my parents right away. My dad will be right over to hear more about it," Joy says with excitement, giving Willis a hug. and then reaching into her back pocket for her phone to call her parents,

"I should give Chelsea and Larry both a quick call," Willis says.

"Chelsea will be so relieved when she hears they caught the killer. "Finally, I can take Archer for walks," Joy said, smiling, then heading back to the kitchen area to make a call to her parents, giving Willis a big hug before rushing to the back to call.

With a frustrated expression on his face, Larry storms in while Willis is on the phone with Chelsea, snatching wires from his pockets and coming straight for him. Did you tell someone?" With Willis still talking to Chelsea on the phone, Larry asked in a loud voice.

Willis tells Chelsea he has to go, ending the phone call.

"Not a word to anyone; why?" Willis responds.

Larry slams the wires on the counter in front of him. Willis looks down at the wires and notices they're parts of Larry's trail camera.

"I stopped to check on my trail camera this morning, and this is what I found. Look at this mess. Some idiot decided it was a smart idea to bash this," Larry says, aggravated, pointing to different parts of the camera and lifting the loose wires hanging from the inside.

"I didn't tell anyone; I kept my word," Willis responds, looking over the broken trail camera parts all over his countertop.

"Whoever did this, and we both know who it is, hit this trail cam at least a dozen times and even took out the SD card. Luckily, they didn't know that my trail cam has a cellular signal, which I paid extra for, so I could receive the footage from my phone. My property is the only area next to the state hospital where you can get any signal at all. I haven't looked at the footage yet, but I'm sure it shows the face of whoever damaged it. I have brought my phone in so we can look at it together and see who was responsible. I'm sorry I came in so angry. I hate it when people mess with my things."

After giving Larry a minute to speak his mind, Willis shared the news.

"The narcotics unit caught Sarah's killer and the person behind the drug problem in the area this morning. It's finally over," Willis said, waiting for Larry's response.

"Over? What's over?" Larry asks, confused.

"This morning, just down the street from here, the narcotics team made the bust. You could probably hear the sirens as you drove into town. We were starting to focus primarily on the Porters, but we were off this whole time; it was Mother Mary behind it all. I can't believe we didn't catch on to Mary's family's involvement even before she returned to town; her son must've been running things while she was away. The whole thing just unraveled over the last couple of days." Willis shares with Larry, still confused by the situation.

"How can this be over? It makes absolutely no sense. How can you believe this? You're smarter than that, Willis," Larry says in frustration, throwing his hands in the air.

"Mary is behind it all, from what the UPSET narcotics team shared. Not just the drug ring, but the killings of Sarah, Noah, and the others." Willis explained.

"Something doesn't line up," Larry replies.

Larry walks around the empty café, trying to wrap his head around what he's hearing and gathering his thoughts.

"What about my trail cam and the Porters then? What's going on in that barn?" Larry asks Willis.

"The Porters may not like you or me, but I don't see how they are involved in this," Willis responds.

"You're telling me everything with the barn, my busted trail cam, Sarah's inheritance, and Thomas Porter trying to scare you at Dollarville Dam is for nothing?" Larry asks with a raised voice.

"Thomas Porter is a harsh alpha male with a superiority complex, but is he a killer, or a drug kingpin? I don't know. Maybe he's all talk, no bite. Let's wait and see what happens with Mary, and leave this up to the courts to handle."

"Look at you just giving up," Larry says, disappointed in Willis' response.

"I'm not giving up. I still want to help find out why someone destroyed your trail camera. I am just glad that whatever is happening on your land has nothing to do with drugs and killings. How about we check out the footage you have?" Willis asks.

"No, I think I'll be fine on my own from here on out," Larry says with a softer than usual voice while picking up the pieces of his trail camera from the counter.

"Oh, come on, Larry, don't get sensitive," Willis says.

"I don't have closure. Something's still off."

"Think of the relief that everyone must be feeling right now around the village, with a level of closure for the families affected by this when they hear the news. At the very least, Mary's victims will have some level of justice and an opportunity to return to a sense of normalcy, whatever that may entail in the future," Willis says to Larry.

"Not this time. When I get home, I will watch whatever video I have stored on my phone.

The only thing I ask, Willis, is don't close this thing off yet in your head; this may not be as over as you think yet," Larry tells Willis with a stern look on his face as he heads towards the exit of Northern Bites.

"Let me know what you find on the video; I'll keep an open mind," Willis says as Larry walks out the door without a response, other than a quick nod as he heads out.

CHAPTER 27

After Noah's death, Willis volunteers to deliver his belongings from the house Noah rented to Noah's family in the Amish community south of Newberry, near Engadine. Over the years, Noah had lost contact with his family, but secretly, he stayed in close contact with his twin sister Bethany, who greeted Willis as he entered the family's farm.

"Thanks for letting me bring these items to you and your family, Bethany. I didn't want Noah's belongings to be thrown away or donated without you getting a chance to see if there's anything you may want to keep. Your brother was a great man and friend," Willis says, handing over a box of Noah's belongings to his sister, Bethany.

"I can smell my brother in these old flannel shirts," Bethany says, holding the shirt close to her nose, wiping away tears, and trying to pull herself together.

Willis starts to head back to his SUV when Bethany asks him not to leave yet.

"I would like you to meet my parents and maybe say something about Noah, if you wouldn't mind. My father's behavior has changed since we received the message from our neighbors about Noah's passing. I think it would mean a lot to them to hear from a friend of Noah's," Bethany says.

"I will do my best," Willis replies.

Willis is escorted by Noah's sister Bethany to her parents, who are watching their animals in their pasture.

Noah's dad reached out and shook hands firmly with Willis. "I see you brought some of Noah's belongings, but we cannot accept them. Our son left us long ago. That person wasn't our son. Noah's father says with a severe expression on his face, "The devil took our son years ago; the world did to him just as we warned him." Noah's mother bowed her head in sorrow.

As Noah's parents leave, her mother puts her hand on her husband's back and expresses her grief. "My father is a great man, just heartbroken. I must honor my father's request and not accept Noah's belongings. I have family in Engadine; you can take the items to them instead. My father will be ready to take those items someday, just not yet." Bethany shares.

"I can understand, and I don't know what I would do if anything ever happened to my son. If you give me the address, I will drop these items by on my way back home, so when your family is ready to view Noah's belongings."

"Thank you. That's very kind of you to come all this way. While you are here, would you like to see some of Noah's favorite spots and hear a story or two?"

"I would," Willis replies.

Willis followed Bethany on a guided tour of her sprawling family farm. "My grandfather, Jonas, was the first of our family to settle here over sixty years ago. It all started with one farm that has grown to eleven families living off this land now."

"This is my father's brother, Jacob's house," Bethany says, pointing to a two-story yellow house next door with children playing volleyball in the grass, the one Amish teenage boy rollerblading on a dirt driveway. In the distance, women sit at a picnic table, weaving, laughing, and enjoying the pleasant weather of the spring day.

"We Amish still know how to enjoy life. I even use a cellphone every once in a while, but it's nice not being chained to technology," Bethany says with a slight smile, watching Willis look on at the children at play.

Bethany walks Willis over to the top of a small hill, where a large oak tree stands all by itself.

"This tree, Noah and I claimed as ours as children. No matter the season, this was our special place. Over the years, we would leave messages on it, and I miss those times." Bethany says this while looking at and touching the oak tree.

With a quick glance at the bark, Willis noticed some tiny hand-carved engravings on the tree.

"I have to ask you something, Bethany. I had plenty of conversations with Noah, and he never clearly shared why he left. Was it for Sarah?" Willis asks.

"No, I wish Sarah was the reason Noah left us. Have you ever heard of Rumspringa?" Bethany asks.

"No," Willis responds.

"During Rumspringa, if you choose, you can leave the community for months to experience life outside when you are around sixteen, but most choose to stay. Noah and his cousin Abraham decided to leave and try the outside world. Friends they made while out in the world during Rumspringa asked Noah one night to grab one of our buggies as a prank to take around Engadine for the night. During the night, Noah and Abraham broke into our sheds and took two horses and a buggy.

While traveling back into town, a drunk driver hit them, killing the horses, destroying the buggy, and injuring them. Days later, Noah and Abraham came before my father, the bishop, and received their punishment at trial in our community. Abraham accepted the punishment, but Noah went into a wild rage, calling out my father in front of everyone, and he walked away and left forever. My father tried to get in touch with Noah, but he never replied. Weeks went by, and without a response, the community

170

voted Noah excommunicated for his actions. Noah possessed a strong, independent spirit and had big dreams. I wish he could have left the right way."

"Did you participate in Rumspringa?" Willis asks.

"No, I stayed. I had already met my husband, Nathaniel, at a young age and never had the desire like Noah to leave the community. This Amish community is filled with amazing people who take care of each other. All I've ever wanted and needed is right here, but for my brother, things were different. I don't think Noah ever felt at home here. Before you leave, can you tell me one thing? Someone told us he had needle marks from drug use on his arm. Did my brother get involved in drugs?" Bethany asks, walking Willis back over towards his vehicle.

"Never. Soon, everyone will know the truth. Even though Noah had a distinct style of doing things, he always had the right intentions. All he wanted to do was build a beautiful life for himself, Sarah, and Ava. Did you know Sarah and Noah got engaged?"

"Oh, I hadn't heard. I hadn't had a chance to talk to my brother since early December," Bethany responds before feeling the grief, knowing that Sarah and Noah were so close to being married and now are both dead.

"I know with everything in me that until Noah's last breath, he was out fighting to find out what happened to Sarah, and now we have the answers for him."

"We Amish tend not to hold on to things in our hearts, but I hope this lady Mary receives the harshest punishment possible. Nothing will bring my brother back, though. I feel like a part of my soul was taken away until we meet again someday."

"If there are any updates about Noah, I promise I will deliver them directly to you and your family. Thanks for sharing the stories about Noah and showing me around your home."

"I'm grateful to share these stories about Noah and me. I don't get to talk about my brother much anymore. Even though we Amish keep to ourselves, we still care deeply about others. Everything that happens affects us all. In our Amish community, we have encountered the pain of missing individuals, leaving behind a haunting emptiness that lingers in the air. Can I give you their names in case you hear anything about them at the trial?" Bethany asks.

"Yes, definitely. I have a notebook in my SUV. I'll go grab it so you can give me those names. If I hear anything about any of those names, I will bring the news to you personally."

CHAPTER 28

As tourist traffic grows with the warming waters and spring fully in swing, Memorial Day weekend approaches. The 'closed' signs from winter flip to 'open' around the area at local businesses and hotels across the village. For the busy season ahead, Willis and Joy hire extra employees. The warm season is short but an extremely popular time of year, with every hotel and campground filled across the Upper Peninsula for weeks on end. These are the months when everyone forgets about the hard, long winters and wants to be a Yooper and enjoy the inland seas. Northern Bites is a well-liked destination for road trippers traveling across the Upper Peninsula, as it is situated directly between the Tahquamenon Falls and the Pictured Rocks National Lakeshore. Visitors can stop here for refreshments and a break.

"The tourists have scared off the locals, I can see," Willis says to Bob and Mike early in the morning in Northern Bites.

"The locals do get a little weird as the trolls come up from below the bridge," Bob says.

"Yoopers are known for their tough skin, but they can be sensitive when an outsider starts messing with one of their own. The drama you stirred up a while back with the Porters, claiming that they weren't the founders of the village, spread quickly around town, which didn't help. That news traveled fast around this small town, even without you saying a thing. People find out things in this village. You realize that half of the village is related to the Porters in some way, and the other half works for them. Now that the murderers and the drug ring have been apprehended, the locals will be coming back in droves." Mike says.

"Locals love to point fingers, just not at themselves. There's a rumor going around the Elks Lodge that you despise the Porters. I try to set them straight, but some are just ignorant. Sadly, no matter what you do to make this village better for some, you will always be an outsider," Bob says, drinking his coffee and looking over at Willis.

"I have a great idea for you, Willis. Why don't you drop by a few dozen of those priceless baked goods some afternoon as a goodwill offering to the Porters' lumber yard? A sign of no hard feelings, and those baked goods can go a long way in this village," Mike replies.

"I know I have to do something, but part of me just can't let go of it till Mary is convicted. Do you really think, after all you've seen over the years with Mary and what you witnessed in Paradise, that Mary was really behind all of this? Willis asked Bob.

"I've seen Mary do a lot of bad things around here for decades, so I wouldn't put this past her. I know Larry comes in and blurts out his theories to you, but don't fall into his conspiracies. That man has some deep hurt from the way he and his father have been treated in the village over the years, so he's jaded about the Porters. In the long run, it will be easier for you and your bakery in Newberry if you move on from this and let the legal system handle it. From the evidence, I've heard that the FBI, narcotics team, and state police have gathered a lot of evidence against her. It sounds like you're heading toward a dead end if you keep looking elsewhere. In just a couple of days, when she's convicted, Newberry and those families affected will finally have their justice."

CHAPTER 29

One morning, after struggling with the idea that Mary might not be the one responsible for the murders for several sleepless nights, Willis saw Rick, his Methodist church pastor, enter Northern Bites. "Great to see you, Pastor Rick; do you have office hours today? I see you have your collar on." Willis says.

"Yeah, some of the ladies of the church wanted to meet about the next pastie bake sale event, which is serious business in this town and one of the biggest fundraisers to support the church. After sitting in that meeting for an hour, I thought I deserved a coffee." Pastor Rick jokingly replies.

"If you can spare a couple of minutes, I would love to talk to you about some things that have been bothering me," Willis replies.

"Come over when you can. I will be in my office at the church."

Willis waited until the noon rush died down, then crossed the street to the Methodist church entrance, which was left unlocked. Willis stepped into the church and stopped for a moment in the empty chapel. He looked up at the crucifixion statue with Christ in the center as he stood in the center walkway of the pews. The bright light of the midday sun was streaming through the stained glass windows, creating colorful light rays that danced across the chapel.

"Stunning, isn't it?" Pastor Rick says, walking into the chapel, he sees Willis staring at Christ on the cross.

"It is. I've always loved the peace you feel when you walk into this chapel. Every Sunday, this is one of the only places where I step away from all the craziness and focus on what really matters with my family," Willis says, looking at the stained glass murals.

"So, what's bothering you, Willis? Did the doctor tell you to switch to decaf coffee?" Pastor Rick jokingly asks.

"Let's pray that day never comes. That would be a dark day. I'm just tired and burnt out," Willis replies, taking a seat on one of the pews.

"I've never had a business, but I bet it can be taxing. Do you take time away from it?" Pastor Rick asks, taking a seat near Willis.

"It's not Northern Bites; it's this village. I can't wrap my head around what to do. The horrible things happening in this village keep me up at night, even with Mary now in custody. I pray and pray again, but I hear nothing back. Everyone around me seems ready to let go, but I can't stop. I feel like it's not over. I don't know why I care so much," Willis says.

"Maybe you are hearing back, but not in the way you would think," Pastor Rick replies.

"Deep down; I know something is off. I just can't place it yet," Willis says.

"I've heard many things in my short time in the ministry. This church is my first pastoral position. I came from Green Bay, so I'm not from the Upper Peninsula either. The minister before me pastored this church for over forty years; they even have a painting of him in the halls. I walk by his picture every day, and I'm reminded that any time something wrong happens, I can hear the whispers of how he would've handled it better, but I know I am here for a purpose. I believe I am here for a reason and will stay till I hear from God. It's my time to move on. Do you believe you're here for a purpose?" Pastor Rick asks.

"I don't know," Willis replies.

"Knowing that I'm called to lead this congregation is what makes me able to stay in ministry. It's emotionally tiring to be a minister. The only way I could do this is beyond my ability. I believe those sleepless nights and constant pull are God trying to talk to you," Pastor Rick replies.

"Sometimes I wonder if I made a mistake coming here instead of staying in Kansas City. I still remember the first time I visited Newberry, seeing all the potential and the natural beauty everywhere you turn. I hear it all the time about how great this town used to be and how the Upper Peninsula is called God's country, but what I see daily is far from it."

"My advice is to listen to that voice and don't run away from what God's telling you to do, no matter how hard it looks."

"Thanks for listening to me rant, Rick; I mean Pastor Rick."

"You can call me Rick any time."

"Rick, it is."

"Just keep listening, Willis."

CHAPTER 30

As Mary's trial approaches, rumors about everything that has happened in her case spread like wildfire throughout the village of Newberry. The victims' families wait patiently to see justice for those killed. Mary's house on Truman Blvd. is off limits, with crime scene tape and signage posted at every corner.

With repeated threats to set Mary's house on fire, there is a lot of tension in the neighborhood, and additional state police support personnel are keeping a close eye on the residence. Back at Northern Bites, as tensions rise as families wait for the verdict of the killings of Sarah and Noah, Willis and Joy try to run things as usual. However, with the town on edge and regional news outlets back in town, nothing is normal.

Two days before the trial, Willis and Joy are running the front counter at Northern Bites, trying to keep their minds off of what's to come. Willis sees Neal for the first time since he came in right after his narcotics team arrested Mary. For the first time, Neal is accompanied by his family and is dressed normally rather than in his usual assortment of disguises.

"Is that the real Neal this time?" Willis asks Neal as his family looks at the menu and baked goods on display.

"This is as real as it gets," Neal responds.

"I prefer the clean-shaven Neal without the beard. I'm so glad it's gone," Neal's wife says with a big smile, touching his clean-shaven face.

"Willis and Joy, this is my wife, Alice, and these two kids running around are our little ones, Eric and Rachel," Neal says, pointing to each family member trying to keep control of his kids running around in excitement.

"Nice to finally meet you all. I didn't know for certain if you were real or part of maybe one of Neal's undercover made-up stories," Willis jokingly responds.

"We are for sure real; it's great to be out as a family again," Neal says, hugging his wife.

"Neal's been with his unit working on this case for over three years but couldn't tell anyone a thing about it. My parents and friends always asked me what Neal was up to," Alice said with a sigh. "But I couldn't tell them. I didn't even know myself. I'm terrible at keeping secrets."

"I suppose we should order," Neal said, checking out the menu. "Can I get four wildberry smoothies and two cinnamon rolls with the maple glaze? Your cinnamon rolls are a hit with our family and Alice's coworkers at the lumberyard she manages."

"Oh yeah?" Willis asked as he started to make the family's orders. "Which lumberyard is that?"

"Porter Hughes Lumber, over in the industrial park next to the prison. My mother was the last of the Hughes, so we could change it to just Porter Lumber now, but I like how it still shares both sides of my family in the name," Alice says, shocking Willis as his back is turned while making their drinks. Willis realizes he's talking with Thomas Porter's daughter.

"Porter Hughes Lumber went almost a century without a single woman in a management position. Even though she's her dad's little princess, Alice had to bust her butt to get where she is today. Now she manages everything at the lumberyard," Neal says, bragging about Alice.

"I just oversee the books, Neal. Joy here is the real princess," Alice said, gesturing to Joy behind the counter next to Willis. She beat me for Homecoming Queen back in the day."

Joy smiled graciously. "It was a long time ago; I was just as surprised as you were that night. I thought you were the queen by a landslide, Alice." Joy replies.

"You won the homecoming queen fair and square," Alice says with a smile.

"Didn't you head down to the University of Michigan in Ann Arbor after graduation?" Joy asks.

"I did, until my grandfather passed away. My dad needed help here, running the yard. I put my degree on hold and headed back to good old Newberry. This town always brings you back. After high school, I remember telling myself I would never return, but that didn't last long. I'm glad I came back, though the lumberyard might not even be here otherwise. My grandfather was an expert with numbers, but my father's gift is more being in the woods, logging, socializing, or hunting. My dad says he still runs the yard and his other businesses in town, but I do all the paperwork so he can have fun with the boys."

Willis was tempted to ask Alice what went on behind the lumberyard in the barn, but he held back. He knew that she might be involved.

"It sounds like your father made the right move. Your family has quite the history around here," Willis says.

"We do. My father takes a lot of pride in our family's name and heritage in Newberry," Alice responds as Willis hands her a smoothie.

"I think we have a fresh batch of cinnamon rolls in the back; let me quickly grab those for you. Nothing beats fresh out of the oven," Willis says, heading to the back with Joy staying in the front, chatting with Alice and Neal.

Willis leaned against the door frame in the kitchen, rubbing his forehead in disbelief. After all this time, he had been telling Thomas Porter's son-in-law, Neal, so much about what he'd heard around town. He was trying to recall what he told Neal before. Willis thought back to all the times he had talked to Neal. He knows this could be his only opportunity to find out what's happening in the barns without actually going inside. Willis must think of a way to ask Alice something that won't make her suspicious. Willis puts the fresh cinnamon rolls on a plate and brings them out to Neal and Alice, who are now sitting with their children at a table.

"I almost forgot to add whipped cream to the smoothies; let me bring that over to you and maybe add a little extra. You can never have too much, right?" Willis asked Neal's kids with giant smiles on their faces.

"Alice, I've always wondered what the lumber world is like up here. I see my father-in-law's sawmill in passing, but how is it navigating the large timber?" Willis asks Alice as he brings over the cinnamon rolls to their table.

"Nothing like it used to be around here., but we have some of the highest quality timber in these woods. My family will do whatever it takes to keep our lumberyard going in Newberry. The recession hit this area hard in 2018, but we fought through it and found some new business connections downstate."

Willis almost asked if they started to use the barn behind the lumberyard but decided he might push too far, so he held back. Willis tells Neal it was great to see the whole family and then walks back into the prep room, grabs his phone, and texts Larry quickly.

Larry: We need to talk. I agree, and I don't think it's over yet. Can you come by Northern Bites? I found out that the undercover agent I've been talking with says that his wife is Thomas Porter's daughter.

Willis waited for a response, then his phone buzzed.

We need to talk. I took a few days off to check on my property in the Copper Country. I looked at the footage from my broken trail camera. and I have some interesting stuff to show you when I get back. Let's meet up at noon at Timber Charlie's.

CHAPTER 31

Two days after Willis and Larry's text conversation, Larry returns to the village to meet Willis. The plow truck crossed into Larry's lane, and he tried to slow down and move to the side of the road to avoid it. However, the plow truck kept coming directly at him. Larry pulled over to the side of the road and quickly tried to unbuckle his seatbelt, but he didn't have enough time to get out of the car before the plow truck collided head-on with Larry's car. The impact of the collision rolled both vehicles into the ditch, and Larry's car landed upside down with him still inside. The front of Larry's truck and the front of the plow truck were melded together. The scene was littered with broken glass, gasoline leaks, and metal. There was a massive mud trail that led to the accident's wreckage. Given how serious the accident was, passersby who witnessed it rushed to assist.

At Northern Bites, Bob rushed in after hearing on his police scanner to inform Willis of Larry's accident.

"Larry was involved in a terrible crash on the M28 highway coming into town a couple of minutes ago. I thought you would want to know. He is in the hospital at the moment, and the wreck sounds like a bad one. If I were you, I would go over quickly." Bob said urgently.

"I was just on my way to catch up with Larry at Timber Charlies. I'm going to run upstairs and tell Joy I'm heading to the hospital, and then I will head right down," Willis responds, rushing off.

After speaking with Joy, Willis raced to the hospital and entered the emergency room.

"Hi, I'm friends with Larry Burke and wanted to check in on how he's doing. I just heard he was in an accident," Willis says to the receptionist.

"What's your name, sir?" asked the receptionist, looking at her computer.

"Willis Davis," Willis responds.

"Mr. Burke has you on his emergency contact list, Mr. Davis. Unfortunately, Mr. Burke is no longer here at our hospital. He was riding in the ambulance to the hospital when the doctors asked that he be transferred. His injuries are too severe to treat here in Newberry, so he was just airlifted to UP Health Systems in Marquette," the receptionist tells Willis.

"Marquette? He must've been in pretty awful shape," Willis replies.

"His condition is life-threatening, so if he is already headed to Marquette, you might want to head there as soon as possible. UP Health can provide you with information as you travel. However, I can't guarantee that you will see him if you drive to Marquette. Based on my brief notes, it's unfortunate to say that Mr. Burke's condition is very critical."

"Thank you," Willis says as he heads quickly out of the hospital.

With only two options, neither of which seemed like a good choice, Willis left the hospital. Rather than wait for updates, Willis decided to check on Larry in Marquette as he drove back home to inform Joy. When Willis arrives at his residence on the second floor of the Newberry Building, he discovers Joy and Archer playing on the living room floor.

"Did you see Larry? Is he okay?" Joy asks, looking up at Willis as she holds Archer while he plays with a toy.

"They airlifted Larry to the hospital in Marquette. I wasn't expecting to be one of Larry's emergency contacts, but with no family left in the area, I guess that's why he added me. I feel like someone needs to go be with him, and I guess that's me." Willis shares with Joy.

"The fog outside should clear soon, and I can get Archer ready so we can go with you. You don't need to do this alone. Archer and I can make the grocery runs while you're checking in on Larry if you want us to come along," Joy says, getting up from the floor and quickly packing things to be with Willis on his ride to Marquette.

As Willis and his family drove past the accident scene, where Larry's car collided with the plow truck, Willis glanced at the tracks left in the field as they drove by, his mind racing with thoughts of what pain Larry must be in right now.

Willis drove through Munising on his way to Marquette. He was reflecting on everything that had happened. He glanced out the window and saw Algar Falls, a waterfall cascading down the side of a cliff near the road. Then he turned and saw a stunning view of Lake Superior. The lake's blue waters glistened in the sun, extending as far as the eye could see.

"Lake Superior feels endless, doesn't it?" Willis asks Joy, glancing out his window at Lake Superior.

"They don't call them the inland seas for nothing," Joy replies, looking out at the crashing waves.

"Is there any news regarding Larry's accident?" Willis asks Joy while she looks down at her cell phone.

"No signal here. I'm just scrolling through old photos. We're getting closer to Marquette, so I should get a signal soon. I hope Larry pulls through this. You and Larry have become pretty close over the last few months. I remember how much he used to drive you up a wall. What changed?" Joy asked.

185

"A year ago, I never would have thought that Larry and I would become good friends. Since we became aware of what was happening and how outsiders we were in Newberry, the small-town politics, drugs, and murders in the community drew us closer as friends. I could not stand him at first. We both think that Newberry's issues must be fixed. Larry is a decent man who wants to do the right thing for the community despite everything. He is just misinterpreted."

"A couple of minutes later, as Willis and his family get closer to Marquette, Archer notices colorful, massive metal creations mixed in with the tall pines and a playground out the SUV's window.

"Dad look. I want to go there. Can we go?" Archer yells excitedly.

"Oh, Lakenenland caught your eye, didn't it, Archer? How about we stop by on our way home, buddy?" Willis asks Archer to get his instant approval.

"Do you believe moving up north was the right decision for us?" Willis asks Joy, looking over at her as he drives along with Lake Superior just outside the window.

"Absolutely," Joy said, putting her hand on Willis's arm. "Just look at how amazing Lake Superior looks right now," Joy said, pointing out the window to the crashing waves on the shoreline on a sunny day. "The water is a brilliant blue, and the waves are so powerful. It's so beautiful here. I know things have been tough lately," Joy said. "But I think better days are coming."

Willis nodded. "I hope so," he said.

Willis pulled into the hospital parking lot and got out of the SUV. He switched seats with Joy, handing her the keys and thanking her for coming with him. Willis gave Joy a kiss and a hug before walking into the hospital to visit Larry. Willis checked in at the front desk and took a seat in the waiting room. He waited patiently for a few minutes, and then a nurse came over to him.

"Hi, are you Mr. Davis?" The nurse asked.

"Yes," Willis replies.

"Mr. Burke is under heavy pain medication, and he's been coming in and out of consciousness. But he's a fighter. I've seen many people give up with far less serious injuries." The nurse shares.

The nurse talks with Willis about the CT results and then leads him down the hall to Larry's room and the emergency wing. Larry had tubes connecting him to medical equipment and was covered in bruises when Willis entered the room. While Willis is looking over at Larry, a doctor enters. "Mr. Burke has a significant brain bleed, so we are attempting to control it and keep him from losing consciousness. Are you a family member?" The doctor asks.

"No, just a friend," Willis replies.

"Your friend, Mr. Burke, is doing most of the work. I wouldn't expect any response, but you never know. Let me know if you notice anything," the doctor says.

Sitting next to Larry, Willis considers how different his day was only hours ago, as well as all the equipment keeping Larry alive. Even though he doesn't know if Larry can hear him, Willis talks to him.

"If you can hear me, Larry, I guess you didn't hate me that much, making me one of your emergency contacts," Willis says jokingly.

Willis waits for some sort of response, but nothing, as Larry just looks asleep in front of him.

"I'm so sorry this happened to you," Willis says after minutes of silence setting by Larry's side. Then Willis notices movement in Larry's fingers on the side of the hospital bed closest to him.

"Can you hear me, Larry?" Willis asks, but there is no response.

"I wish we could've met at Timber Charlie's. You could have told me everything you discovered and observed with that trail camera. I don't know if I can do this on my own."

Willis notices Larry trying to open his eyes slightly, like he's trying to respond.

"Larry, can you hear me?" Willis asks Larry loudly, shocked to see another response.

A part of Larry's mouth begins to move as he emerges from the induced coma.

Willis yells down the hospital hallway, attempting to draw the attention of the medical staff, "He is trying to respond right now." Willis turned back around to Larry, but what he saw made his heart stop. Larry was on his bed, convulsing, his vital signs rapidly increasing. The alarms were blaring, and the nurses were rushing into the room.

A nurse shouts, "He's coding," checking Larry's vital signs as other nurses hurriedly enter the room.

"He was moving his finger and his eyes, and I think he was trying to tell me something," Willis says frantically to the nursing staff and doctors rushing around him to Larry.

The nurse turned to Willis. "I'll have one of our nurses take you back to the waiting area," she said. "His levels are off the charts, so we'll have to move him into the emergency room to get them back down right now."

Willis nodded in a daze. "Okay," he said.

Willis stands in shock, watching the nurses roll Larry down the hallway in front of him to the emergency room as time has slowed to a screeching halt.

Willis feels a buzz in his pocket—a text from Joy, he sees.

Joy: We just finished shopping and will be outside when you are ready. Tell Larry I'm praying for him. Archer can't stop talking about Lakenenland.

Willis: I'll be right down; they just had to rush Larry back to the emergency room.

Willis comes down to his SUV and gets into the passenger seat.

"How serious is it?" Joy asks.

"I don't think my coming in to visit helped at all. I was only in the room with Larry for a couple of minutes, and he was unresponsive, but as I continued to talk, Larry attempted to respond. Larry was trying to communicate something to me, but then his levels spiked."

"Lakenenland!" Archer excitedly yells from the back seat.

"Lakenenland, here we come," Willis replies, turning back to look at Archer in the back seat with a smile.

"Are you sure you will be okay with leaving?" Joy asked.

"I'll be fine. I only made things worse for Larry coming to visit," Willis replies.

Joy entered Lakenenland, and her eyes scanned the vibrant welded metal creations scattered across the landscape, with Archer glued to the windows in excitement at every passing colorful metal structure. Willis tried to find solace in the moment. However, his mind couldn't stop dwelling on the unsettling scene he had witnessed at the hospital.

As they reach the end of Lakenenland, Joy parks the SUV, with Willis getting out and taking Archer to a playground to get some energy out. Watching Willis and Archer play on the swings, Joy settles down on a picnic bench to relish the quiet family time. Joy's phone rings in her purse as she watches. After opening her purse, Joy answers the phone. On the other end of the line is her mother. As Willis keeps pushing Archer on the swing set, he hears the faint sound of Joy's phone ringing and sees her in distress. After hanging up the phone, Joy approaches Willis slowly while wiping away her tears. "What's wrong?" Willis asks, his eyes wide with fear, his grip on Archer's swing coming to a halt. The air around them feels heavy with the weight of his words.

Joy says, her voice hardly audible and her eyes filling with tears, "It is my father."

"Oh no," Willis responds, his voice soft and filled with sorrow. The scent of smoke lingers in the air, a constant reminder of the tragedy unfolding.

"My father's sawmill is on fire," Joy continues, her voice trembling as tears stream down her face.

"Most of it has already burned to the ground," she adds, her words carrying the weight of loss. Willis instinctively pulls Joy closer, offering comfort and solace amidst the chaos.

"Let's get to your parents right away," Willis says urgently.

CHAPTER 32

Willis quickly drives back to Ted's mill to be with Joy's parents after the fire at the sawmill. As Willis and his family arrive on the road to Ted's sawmill, they can see the smoke from the fire high above the trees. Willis turns toward the dirt road to Ted's and sees a fire truck leaving Ted's sawmill. As they park the SUV, Joy rushes over to her mother.

"Mom, we got here as soon as possible. I can't believe this happened," Joy says, hugging Ruth and looking around, seeing what's left of the sawmill covered in ashes.

"I'm glad no one was in the mill when it happened; if Ted was working inside, he wouldn't have made it out alive. The sawmill went up in flames with all this wood around. It's a total loss, as you can see. There wasn't much the Fire Department could do when they arrived, other than spray down part of the fire still burning to control it from expanding. The mill burned down so fast; I've never seen anything like it. Poor Ted just had to stand by and watch it all happen," Ruth says, looking over at Ted, who was slowly walking around what was left of the sawmill, looking for anything salvageable.

"Poor Dad, he must be broken over this," Joy replies, looking at her father.

"We just finished eating dinner, and we're about to start on a puzzle when we smelled the smoke, so we walked outside thinking one of the neighbor's homes was on fire. All you could see was the black clouds of smoke coming from the mill," Ruth replies.

"I can't believe my dad is crying; this is the only time I've seen my father ever cry," Joy says to Willis and Ruth standing next to her, looking at Ted rubbing his eyes, bending down, wiping away the tears, and picking up what's left of his cutoff saw in the soaked ash-covered concrete slab.

Joy walks over to her father to be with him.

"Let's go back to the house, Dad," Joy said, putting her hand on Ted's shoulder as he touches what's left of some wood he just cut the day before.

"All this equipment was put together in my mill over decades. My insurance can cover the replacement of equipment, but not these pieces. Although some of the equipment is outdated, it functions much better for me than any new equipment ever could. Breaking in the new equipment will take years. I don't have time like that left in me. With my old mill saws, I could make a clean cut on a log, even with a blindfold over my eyes. There is no way I can build this sawmill again like I did. It's over," Ted shares with Joy.

"You still have your chainsaw at the house, Dad, and hundreds of acres to spend time in the woods," Joy responds, trying to be optimistic for her father.

"I do still have that; thanks, honey," Ted responds to Joy's hopeful words, standing back up slowly.

Willis watches Joy and Ted have a moment together alone, giving them space. He can see in Ted's eyes the loss, like a piece of his soul has been taken from him.

"It's one thing to plan out letting go of something, but another to have it ripped away from you," Ted says as he walks towards Willis with some parts of his former cut saw in his hand, with his entire body soaked from digging through the ash-filled water and from the drips from the burnt metal from the fire hose.

With Joy and Archer by his side, Ted walked silently past Ruth on his way back to their home. The search for anything of value left from the sawmill ended. Willis walked over to Ruth, still looking on in disbelief at the complete loss of the sawmill.

"I'm so sorry, Ruth," Willis said. "I can't believe this happened."

"I don't understand how this fire started," Ruth said. "Ted swears he turned everything off in the mill before he left a couple of hours ago. His memory isn't as good as it used to be with turning off things, but in other things, he's still as sharp as a tack. Everything was turned off; it doesn't make any sense." Ruth shares, shaking still over the stress of the moment.

"I don't know either," Willis said. "But we'll figure it out."

"How about I look around and see if there's anything else salvageable or that I think Ted would want in the debris?" Willis said. "You should go be with Ted and warm up Ruth; I know this is difficult for you too. If I find anything in the debris, I'll bring it back with me," Willis says to Ruth.

Ruth doesn't say a thing but leans over, gives Willis a giant hug, and then walks back to her home.

Willis walks around the soaked slab covered in ash, softly moving over debris, looking for anything he could salvage for Ted. As he digs through the rubble, Willis notices something dangling in a tree, blowing in the wind in the distance. As Willis walked closer to the tree, he recognized that it was part of Larry's trail camera, with a white note hammered through it by a nail. Willis questions how this ended up on Ted's land, given that only he saw the hanging note. He wondered if Ted and the fire department was too busy trying to put out the fire and clear the debris to look for anything in the woods. With small pieces of Larry's trail camera still attached, Willis removes the note from the tree. Willis opened the note, his heart racing. Someone wrote it in bold marker, and it only contained two words.

"*Last warning.*"

Willis's breath caught in his throat as a surge of uncertainty washed over him. His heart pounded in his chest, its erratic rhythm matching the whirlwind of thoughts racing through his mind. Willis stood frozen, his body tense with indecision, unsure of how to process the overwhelming wave of emotions crashing over him.

Willis gripped the note, a wave of confusion washing over him. He didn't know who to trust. There was no local law enforcement around, and Larry was in the emergency room fighting for his life. Willis started making his way to Ted's house to share the note with him and the rest of the group. But suddenly he changed his mind, as the day had been long and emotionally exhausting. Willis folded up the note and placed it in his back pants pocket, with the full intention of sharing it with Ted as soon as the chaotic moment had subsided. But he couldn't help but wonder who had sent it and what they meant by "last warning."

Willis wondered whether the Porters would take such an action. Willis felt a chill go down his spine. If this didn't stop, he didn't want to consider the consequences for his family or his business being targeted next. He knew something had to be done, but what? Willis needed to devise a plan quickly. If he didn't stop them, what level would they reach?

CHAPTER 33

After weeks of closed hearings, the jury in Mary's trial has finally reached a verdict. The streets are filled with news trucks from across the region, and local vehicles surround the courthouse. The most sought-after seat in the village is the one in the courtroom for the reading of the verdict. Willis arrived early to secure a seat. The trial had been happening behind closed doors until now, and he was eager to hear the jury's decision. Willis went through security and got the last remaining seat in the back row of the courtroom. He looked around the room to see who he recognized. There were many local business owners and council members, as well as Joe from the reservation and other tribal members. Even Mary's youngest son, Ethan, was sitting behind the defense table. Although Ethan was not a part of the drug bust, he might as well have been given the looks and remarks that the people in the courtroom directed at him.

The judge appeared in the courtroom, and the room fell silent. The court's rules and the events of the day were explained to the attendees by the judge. Then Mary's defense team arrived, as well as the prosecutors. Mary entered, handcuffed and dressed in an orange jail uniform. The sound of chains rattling on the wooden floor echoed through the courtroom as Mary entered, flanked by her lawyers. She kept her head down, refusing to make eye contact with anyone. As she walked, the chains on her feet clanked together, creating a loud, jarring noise. The sound seemed to fill the room, drawing everyone's attention to Mary.

Some people in the courtroom stared at her with curiosity or disgust. Others looked away, unable to bear the sight of her.

Mary finally reached the defense table and sat down. Her lawyers whispered to her for a few minutes, and then she stood up and faced the judge.

A man in the middle of the crowd stood up and shouted, "Killer!" at Mary. The judge banged his gavel and yelled.

"Enough!" Guards escorted the man out of the courtroom as the judge declared, "My courtroom will not tolerate any more outbursts of any kind."

The judge called the court to order, and the jury foreman stood up to read the verdict.

"On the charges of possession of illegal substances and trafficking, the jury finds Mary Weber guilty. On the charges of homicide by four individuals, the jury foreman stood up and read the verdict in a clear voice. We, the jury, find the defendant, Mary Weber, guilty on all counts."

The verdict of guilty on all counts is read as Willis looks on at Mary, who is standing with a hopeless expression on her face. The people watching the verdict read in the courtroom erupted into applause, but Willis could only stare at Mary. She stood with a hopeless expression on her face. Willis's gut told him that Mary was being framed, but the evidence against her was overwhelming. He knew that Mary was innocent, but he didn't know how to prove it. Watching the room in celebration, Willis almost feels sick, still unable to believe Mary is guilty. Willis's gut tells him that Mary's involvement is somehow a cover-up, and she's being used as a scapegoat. However, all evidence found at Mary's home, whether real or planted, points to her guilt.

As the celebration continues, the judge leaves the courtroom through a side doorway opened by the bailiff. Willis looks on as Mary gets up from her chair, shaking, with her lawyers helping her stand as she is to be turned over to the guards. The bailiff who escorted the judge out of the courtroom quickly meets with other officers at the courthouse entrance, urgently discussing something Willis notices. As two officers started to take Mary away and those in public seating continued to celebrate, Willis noticed Mary's son, Ethan, sitting motionless as those in the courtroom celebrated around him.

He stood up and held his cell phone in the air above his head, his index finger hovering over the screen.

"Stop!" Ethan screams at the top of his lungs. "Right here, with one tap, I can blow this courtroom up if anyone tries anything, so sit back in your seats and listen to me."

"Ethan, stop! Don't do this!" Mary shouted while being escorted out of the courtroom by two officers, who abruptly halted.

The officers quickly turned, pulling out their pistols and pointing them at Ethan.

"I'll do it; put those guns down now!" Ethan screams again.

The officers slowly lower their weapons, placing them on the ground in front of them to avoid alarming Ethan further.

"You and I both know that someone planted this evidence, but you are too afraid to stand up and say anything. You know my mother had nothing to do with it. I'm not saying any of us are angels, but hear me out. All my mom wanted was to spend the last months of her life with her family. You've stolen that from us, so I'm going to take it away from all of us."

"I'll be okay, son," Mary said, looking over at Ethan with a somber expression. "This isn't the way."

197

"Mama, I love you, but this is the only way. These people hate you. They'll never get it. It's not fair. None of you know what she had to do to get out of prison. All of you should thank her," Ethan said to the people in the courtroom.

Using a side door, the police slowly move into the room behind Ethan without him noticing, trying to find the right angle to take him down until the wood floor of the courtroom cracks. Ethan turns around and sees the police officers.

"Don't take another step. I'm not kidding around!" Ethan yells, looking at the guards and holding his finger closer to his phone's screen. The police freeze in place as the crowd around them shudders in fear, afraid to move.

"This is the only way for you to listen to someone like me. I don't want to hurt anyone, but you need to hear the truth. I'm doing this for you, Mama. Taking over the courtroom like this is the only way I could get you free. Since I have everyone's attention, do you want to know who is destroying our village and my family? I have nothing left to lose. I'm not afraid to share, so I'll tell you who it is," Ethan says loudly in a panic.

As Ethan started to say who he had figured out was behind the killings and the drug ring, the bailiff fired a shot into his hand, hitting the hand holding the phone. Ethan cried out in pain and dropped the phone. The crowd in the courtroom immediately burst out of the room, running and screaming through the exit. Willis stopped at the door and looked back. He saw the guards taking Mary out of the courtroom as she tried to reach her son through the security officers. Ethan was lying on the ground alone. He was in pain, clutching his blood-covered hand. The EMTs pushed through the crowd to attend to Ethan's injury.

As Willis leaves the courthouse, he receives a text from Joy.

Joy: Are you okay? I just got an emergency alert on my phone that there was a bomb threat at the courthouse. I love you so much. Please text me back.

Willis: I'm safe. It was Mary's son, Ethan, who made the bomb threat. I'll explain everything as soon as I get home.

CHAPTER 34

With Mary's conviction, the environment in Newberry changed quickly. The most anticipated weekend of the year, Independence Day Weekend, was just around the corner, and the town was usually bustling with activity. Independence Day Weekend is one of the busiest weekends in Newberry every summer. One of the most significant events in the area is the Paul Bunyan Lumberjack Festival, held around the 4th of July. This small village becomes as busy as Newberry can handle, with pastie sales, pancake breakfasts, and the biggest little parade in the world, just down the road from Newberry in Curtis. All the Independence Day Weekend events ultimately culminate in the Independence Day Parade in Newberry, with each float in the parade showcasing a patriotic theme. Every year, Newberry ends the parade with a final float that features a thirty-foot Paul Bunyan and his blue ox, Babe, encircled by American flags. You will never see more flannel worn in the summer than during this parade weekend. The village even passed a millage years ago to build a metal warehouse just for storing Paul Bunyan and Babe, protecting them from vandalism and the weather. For many locals, seeing these two figures has become a religious experience.

Joy and Willis wisely decided to bring in additional staff for the weekend rush during the parade. As the rush winds down, Willis takes a break from Northern Bites during a slow time. He steps outside with his family to enjoy the end of the parade. The final floats are almost in view.

Willis walked over and stood next to Joy and the rest of her family. They were all gathered on the sidewalk, waiting for the Paul Bunyan float to pass by. Willis could see the float in the distance, and it was quickly approaching. The two Newberry fire trucks come through right before the last floats. As Willis picks up his son Archer onto his arms, water sprays his whole family from the hoses on the fire truck. Joy's ninety-year-old grandmother, Betty, even gets soaked, taking the drenching with a smile in her wheelchair. Willis looks on at Betty, relishing the moment and hoping to enjoy life like Betty when he reaches her age. Joy put her head on Willis's shoulder, looking up at him, smiling. Willis smiled back, but his mood quickly changed when he saw Ava, Sarah's daughter, standing with Chelsea's mother across the street. Willis noticed she appeared lonely. Her face showed signs of struggle as she tried to cope with her grief by missing Noah and Sarah by her side. He wondered how different this day would have been if Noah and Sarah were still alive, standing by her side.

"Wow, look how big that blue cow is, Daddy!" Archer says as he taps Willis's arm, taking his attention away from Ava across the street. While observing the Paul Bunyan float, Willis spots Thomas Porter. Thomas Porter waves to the crowd with enthusiasm at the center of the float Behind him, a colossal American flag flutters in the wind. Thomas Porter's family waved and smiled while standing next to him, looking like they were running for a political office or were part of a royal family. Thomas Porter waves with a giant smile. He holds his wife in his arms, as if nothing has happened. It's as if he had no part in the problems across Newberry. Willis makes eye contact with Thomas Porter, whose facial expression becomes serious as they stare at each other, as Willis knows that Thomas Porter is somehow to blame for Sarah's death and has gotten away with it. As the float moves past Willis and the parade ends, Willis remembers Ava standing across the street and looks over to find her no longer there. At that moment, Willis realized that unless he could somehow link Thomas Porter to the murders and the drug ring, nothing would ever be able to remove the cloud hanging over Newberry and give him peace of mind. He had to find out if anything had ever happened in that barn, even if it meant going alone. Larry was fighting for his life, and Willis couldn't ask him for help.

Just then, Joy came up to Willis, soaking wet from the firehouse. She gave him a big hug, breaking him out of his thoughts.

"I'm soaked. Come on, Willis, let's go change so we can enjoy a late lunch with my sisters and my parents at The Lumberjack Luncheon," Joys says, taking Willis's hand and running back into Northern Bites to dry off.

Willis and his family change into dry clothes and close down Northern Bites for the rest of the day. They then drive to the Lumberjack Luncheon at the Tahquamenon River. It is the annual follow-up to the parade. They park in the overflow parking area in a grass field because the main parking lot is full. Joy's sister waves at her to signal that they have a table. The crowd at the Lumberjack Luncheon was eating heartily, their plates piled high with ribs, corn on the cob, watermelon, pasties, and coleslaw. The Lumberjack Luncheon had just finished the finals of the annual log-cutting competition, and the excitement was still in the air. After reading the competition results to the audience, a woman dressed in a Paul Bunyan costume stepped up to the stage and spoke into a microphone. She was holding a sealed envelope in her hand.

"Now we will announce the winner of this year's best pastie award," the woman said. She continued, "Usually, the former champion would present the award. However, last year's winner, Larry Burke, is still fighting for his life after a recent accident. Let's take a moment to say a silent prayer." The woman bowed her head, and everyone else at the luncheon followed her lead. Willis, however, looked around the room. His eyes darted from person to person. He felt rattled by the moment. Willis had to find the truth for Larry, Ava, Sarah, Noah, Ted, and Newberry, so he needed to find out what's really happening in the barn.

"I think I'm going to head back home," Willis says abruptly to Joy after the prayer time ends.

"We just got here; you can't be serious," Joy responds, making up Archer's plate.

"I'm just exhausted from the morning. I would love to chat with everyone, but I really need to go back and rest so I have energy for the fireworks tonight."

Joy knew that Willis was holding something back. She could tell by the way he was fidgeting and avoiding eye contact.

"Is everything okay?" Joy asks.

"Everything is fine," Willis smiles at Joy. Deep down, he knows he isn't okay. Thoughts of what's happening in that barn cloud his mind. He doesn't want her to worry, so he keeps it to himself.

Willis quickly finished his meal and left the luncheon as the area became lively with the start of an axe-throwing competition. Willis walked to his vehicle. He thought about how and when he would reach the barn. He also pondered what he would need.

Willis went home and gathered items to search the barn before Joy and Archer returned. On his way to his room to pack a few things, Willis notices a flier on the chair by his television for the fireworks tonight. It occurs to him that tonight is a perfect time to see what's in the barn. Everyone in the area will watch the fireworks at the Luce County Airport. Willis walks down to the kitchen, looking around for anything he can take as a weapon just in case, and sees a large cutting knife. After putting the knife in his backpack, Willis runs to his SUV's trunk to store his backpack and then goes back up to his bed to take a nap before Joy comes home. As Willis lays his head down to rest, he contemplates how to get to the barn alone tonight, realizing it needs to be before the fireworks in the daylight.

"Daddy, we're back!" Archer yells, and Willis hears his son running up the stairs and the door chime. Archer leaps onto Willis as he is lying in bed after running into his bedroom.

In Willis's arms, Archer exclaims, "I ate three whole corn on the cobs, two full watermelons, and almost a whole cherry pie by myself."

"Two whole watermelons!" Willis responds, looking both excited and shocked.

"Your son might be exaggerating a little," Joy said, walking into the room. "But we did eat too much. I hope we didn't wake you up from your nap. Mind if we join you?"

"Not at all," Willis responds.

Joy joined Willis and Archer on the bed, with Archer snuggled up between them. They all closed their eyes and fell asleep, content to be together.

CHAPTER 35

After a long afternoon nap, Willis drove to Ted's house for an early dinner with Joy's whole family before the fireworks. After parking, Joy asked Willis to help Archer out of the car. She said she would get the bags from the trunk. Willis remembered his backpack was in the trunk, half-zipped. He also remembered the kitchen knife sticking out too large for the backpack, next to the food they brought for dinner. Willis hurried out of the SUV and reached the trunk before Joy. After hastily covering his backpack, he unbuckled Archer. Archer immediately ran inside after spotting his cousins through the kitchen window. Willis grabbed the box of food and carried it inside.

"What's wrong with you? Something's going on. Why won't you just tell me?" Joy asked, realizing he's still acting off.

"I just needed that nap. I feel a lot better."

As Willis and his family settled in with Joy's family, there was a bustle of activity around the dinner table. Everyone was eager to eat, and they were all waiting anxiously for Ted to say grace.

The dinner table was filled with food, and the smells were intoxicating. There was fried chicken, mashed potatoes, green beans, cornbread, and a variety of pies for dessert.

Willis's stomach growled as he looked at the food. He had been looking forward to this dinner all day.

Finally, Ted stood up and said grace.

"Let's say grace," Ted said. Everyone bowed their heads as Ted prayed.

"Dear Lord, we thank you for all you've given us. Thank you for this gracious dinner. We are so grateful for the food on our table and for the opportunity to be together as a family. We bless this food in Jesus' name. Amen," Ted took a seat, and everyone started passing the food around the table.

Willis looked around at the people he loved, and he felt a wave of gratitude. I am grateful for his family.

As Willis eats and talks with his family, he looks over at Ted, who is sitting at the end of the table. Even after his sawmill burned down a few feet away, Willis could not help but think about everything Ted had been through and how thankful he was for what he still had. Any doubt that Willis still held vanished, knowing that redemption would come for Ted and everyone who had ever been hurt by the Porter and Hughes families in the past in just a few hours. If everything worked out as planned, this area would be like Ted remembered during the glory days of Newberry. No more death, cars on fire, drug deals, or hidden secrets.

As everyone prepared to leave for the fireworks after dinner, Willis realized that he needed to tell Ted something, just in case anything happened to him Looking into the next room, he saw Ted at his computer. He walked over to Ted and asked,

"Ted, can I borrow you away for a minute?"

Ted got up from his computer and followed Willis outside, away from the noise of the room.

"Sure. What's going on?" Ted asked.

Willis took a deep breath. "Ted, I know you didn't burn down your mill," he said.

"I know I saw the cut wire the next day," Ted said.

"I didn't tell you this before, but when I walked around the mill after you left, I found a note that said 'final warning' on it. I think the people who started the fire posted it." Willis shares.

"What?" Ted asked, his eyes widening. "Why didn't you tell me?"

"I didn't want to worry you," Willis said. "The fire was tough enough that day. But I believe Mary was wrongly accused of the murders and that Thomas Porter had a part in burning down your mill. I'm heading to get the evidence right now at the barn next to the State Hospital. I haven't told Joy about this, but I needed to tell someone I could trust where I am going."

"You don't have to do this, Willis. I'll be fine; it's just things; no one was hurt," Ted replies, looking at Willis.

"I feel like I do, though, for Sarah, you, and everyone else in Newberry," Willis replies.

"What do you think you'll find?" Ted asked. "There's no way to walk into that barn on prison grounds. What would anyone do in a place like that? I bet the roofs are about to cave in, not having been touched in years."

"I believe the Porter's smashed Larry's trail cam weeks ago because we were getting close to finding out what was going on in the barn. The video showed people going into the barn at night, but not from the prison; they were coming from their lumberyard. I'm going to investigate. It could be nothing, but it could also be something important," Willis shared.

"I wouldn't do that. One of those guards could have a trigger-happy finger if they see someone messing around on the prison grounds." Ted tells Willis that he is worried about his safety.

"I just want to take a quick peek inside before seeing the fireworks with everyone else," Willis said.

"I don't know about this, Willis," Ted said. "But if you're going to do this, I want to give you something. I have a rifle I've kept since I was a Marine. It's up in my room. I keep it in proper working condition, as you never know when you might need it. Have you ever shot a gun?" Ted asked.

Willis tells Ted, "No, I don't need a gun. I just want to look inside the barn and see what's in there. I'm heading to the barn now. Don't worry; if Joy asks, tell her I went to check on something, and I'll meet everyone at the fireworks."

Ted asks, "I hope you're wrong about Thomas Porter. That man has never seemed to care much for me. Are you sure you don't want me to come along? I won't slow you down, Willis. These old legs can move quickly when needed. I can keep an eye out for you."

"I'll be back with you all in no time," Willis tells Ted, trying to convince him he'll be fine.

"Joy can see through me like her mother can, so hurry back."

"I will. The barn could be nothing or everything," Willis says.

Ted and Willis walked back inside, where Willis noticed Joy and her sisters occupied with a board game. Then he saw Archer sitting on the floor, playing with toy blocks in his hands, next to his cousin's building project. Willis walked over to Archer and kissed him on the top of his head.

"What are you building, buddy?" Willis asked.

Archer remarked, "A house for my robots."

"That's great," Willis said. "I love building things too."

Willis and Archer chatted about building things briefly. Then Willis gets up to leave. As he walks away, he reflects on how lucky he is to be a father. He glances at Joy and wants to tell her he loves her one more time before leaving, but seeing her so engrossed in her board game with her sisters having the time of her life, he just heads out the door not to ruin the moment.

Willis started his SUV, knowing his decision might be foolish. He pulled out of Ted's driveway and glanced at the living room window as he drove past slowly. He saw Joy talking to Ted and wondering where Willis had gone. Willis felt determined as he set out to find evidence and answers, ignoring the potential danger. He gripped the steering wheel tightly, preparing himself for what lay ahead. He was resolute in his mission to uncover the truth.

CHAPTER 36

Willis drove into the industrial park Along with a few other businesses closed on Independence Day, he passed Porter's lumberyard. He parked behind a dumpster. Willis reached over to the passenger seat and grabbed his cell phone and a baseball cap. Opening the trunk, he unzips his backpack and takes out a flashlight and a kitchen knife. He slid them into the inside pocket of his jean jacket.

Willis moved slowly through the tall grass field and the warehouses. He was careful to avoid being seen as he made his way onto the state hospital grounds. His destination was the barn, but he kept a vigilant eye out for any potential onlookers.

The sun set, urging Willis to quicken his pace. Finally, he reached the side of the barn, next to a surprisingly enormous silo. He peeked around the corner of the barn. He discovered that there was no one in view. As the sun began to set, the sound of the wind became more intense. As he approached the front door of the barn, he spotted two big padlocks. Willis knew the padlocks blocked the only entrance he knew about and that they were hidden in the shadows in the trail camera footage. Willis looked around for another way into the barn, but there wasn't another entrance. He thought that his mission was over before it even started. Willis knew he couldn't quit now, no matter what, so he moved around the back of the barn. He didn't know what he was stepping into, since this side of the barn was off-limits, so he moved cautiously. When he reached the back of the barn, he saw that there was a concrete wall with no entrance. But then he noticed a broken window large enough for him to enter. Willis did his best not to make a sound as he crawled through the broken windows. His shoelace caught on a large piece of broken glass, and it fell to the floor, shattering and echoing through the barn. Willis held his breath, listening for any sign someone had heard the noise, but there was no sound. He felt his way through the low-lit hallways, which were filled with the smell of old pipes, dust, and rust. He decided he was far enough inside the barn away from any windows, so it was worth the risk of turning on his flashlight. He peered about the barn with the flashlight on and was astounded by the size of its interior, feeling never-ending. Even with the flashlight, Willis used his hand to feel against the rough concrete walls.

Willis reached a doorway and walked into another room, even larger than the last. There were no walls to touch as he moved forward, just the light from his flashlight in front of him. The room was bare. It felt like total darkness, except where the light shone. Willis kept his free hand out so he didn't run into anything that might be out of his line of sight. He walked around the room for a few minutes, the beam of. his flashlight cutting through the darkness. Willis walked through the large room, bumping his right shoulder and scraping it. He turned his flashlight to his right, revealing the source of the hit by an enormous pile of lumber. Willis looked at the stack of lumber and felt disappointed. He hoped to find evidence of illegal activity by the Porters in the barn. However, the barn looks like it's serving as another storage area. So far, there has been no sign of any illegal activity happening there. Willis considered heading back out of the barn having already taken longer than he originally planned. But he decided to keep searching around for a few more minutes. As Willis walked forward, he continued touching the lumber in case he overlooked something in the log pile. Then he felt something odd in one of the logs; inside the log was a deep hole, cut in a square shape. It looked like it was used to store something in the logs, which was odd in itself, but especially considering the placement of the hole in what feels like the center of the log. Willis felt inside several other logs, noticing the same hole type. In one of them, he felt a small plastic sandwich-sized storage bag filled with a white powdery substance.

Willis found a bag and took multiple photos of it, as well as pictures of the log stacks and holes. He took the photos with his phone and used his flashlight to make things visible. He moved through the room, trying his best to collect evidence. Willis saw some light to his right as he went by the end of the log pile. He headed that way, hoping he was reaching the front of the barn or another way to exit so he wouldn't have to climb back out through the broken window. Willis was looking up at the ceiling with his flashlight, still moving forward, to see if anything was being stored up there. Suddenly, he fell through a hole below him. He hits the ground below hard, feeling like he had fallen a full floor level down and hurting his arm. In the fall, Willis lost his flashlight, hearing it fall apart into pieces all around the room in the darkness. Willis realized he could use his phone's flashlight feature, which wasn't as strong but would at least help him get out of wherever he was now and out of the building. Willis uses the light to look around the new area he is in. He looked up to see the hole he had fallen into and noticed a small ladder on one side of the opening.

As Willis cleaned the dust off from the fall, he saw something else in the middle of the room: an untied single pink shoe that looked identical to the one Sarah left in the woods that the search teams located. Sarah's shoe sat next to a flipped metal chair. Willis took close-up images of the shoe and chair for evidence. A wave of sadness washed over Willis as he realized this dark, cold room was one of the last places Sarah had been alive before being taken to Paradise with the others killed in the fire. Willis searched the room for evidence. He found several clothing items and belongings left behind by other missing people. Willis took picture after picture of everything he could. However, he paused when he picked up one of Noah's business cards and his favorite beanie, both damp and dirty on the floor. He had found what he was looking for, but it came at a high cost. Willis knew he had to get out of the barn fast to give the state police this evidence, even though he was shocked by what he had found in the basement. With his thoughts now on getting out of the barn, Willis made his way back to the ladder he had seen leading to the main floor. As he turned to the ladder, he could see that it was partially disconnected from the opening and would break if he attempted to climb it. He would have to find another way out. Willis walked over to a large plastic cooler he saw while taking pictures with his phone, thinking he could use it as a step to get high enough to pull himself up. As he started to pull it over, he realized the container must be filled, as it was heavy. He opened it and found piles of zip-lock bags inside. Each bag was labeled with different amounts of cocaine, meth, and other drugs. The bags filled the cooler to the top. Willis took more images and realized that the flashlight on his phone was quickly draining the battery. He tried to send the images to Joy from his phone, but there was no signal in the basement. Willis knew these images could validate everything he and Larry had been researching. If he could send the images, it would expose Thomas Porter and the others involved.

Willis pushes over the large cooler on its side, spilling out all the drugs on the floor and taking the weight out of the cooler. He steps up on the cooler, then jumps up and grabs the edges of the opening. He lifts himself up slowly, struggling to climb out awkwardly. Willis pulls himself to the top of the ladder and listens. From the front door of the barn, he hears locks and chains moving. Willis turns off his phone and navigates quietly by pressing against the lumber piles in the opposite direction of the front door. He slips quietly to the other side of the lumber against a wall. Willis waits silently to hear what happens next.

"Come out, come out, wherever you are," said a raspy male voice that sounded like Thomas Porter. The door to the barn creaked open, and Porter stepped inside.

Willis can hear two distinct sets of footsteps walking around the room. While the two walk further into the barn, Willis remains silent, watching them turn on flashlights as they lose the limited sunlight left at the doorway. Willis stays in place, not wanting to run into anything that would draw attention to him. He remembered that Thomas Porter had a reputation for his love of guns, and all Willis had in his jean jacket was a large kitchen knife. As Willis hears the footsteps move closer, he knows that he's outskilled and outnumbered. Willis's only option is to create a diversion and run for the front entrance.

"I'm disappointed it got to this point, boy. Even with the hat on, I could tell it was you, Willis. You don't think Larry was the only person with that idea of trail cameras, do you?" Thomas Porter says it loudly in an arrogant tone.

As Porter and the other man with him get closer and closer, Willis moves further backward, trying to keep his distance.

"This could have ended differently, but you know you will not make it out of this barn alive. If you come out now, maybe you can save your family. My son Doug has been interested in your wife for a while. Porter tries to play on Willis's feelings by saying, "She will make a great Porter wife when you are gone." Willis tries to move in the opposite direction of the voices, slowly moving himself backwards in the large barn, but bumps against a concrete wall behind him. Trapped. Willis needs to figure out a way to bypass Thomas and the other man.

"Let's just end this game of hide-and-seek," says right next to the logs that Willis is hiding behind and past him. Unable to find him, Porter shouts, "You're making me miss the fireworks."

Willis quietly waits as Porter walks farther away, not noticing him. Willis looks around the room for a way out with limited light. Feeling around the floor close by, Willis's fingers touch a metal pipe in front of him. He picks it up and then throws the metal pole to the opposite side of the room from the barn entrance. The metal pole hits the concrete wall hard across the barn, making a loud echo throughout the barn.

The man and Thomas Porter both fired gunshots in the direction of the noise. Footsteps pounded in response from their feet, rushing towards the direction of the shot.

"You had better have shot him, idiot; go check." An enraged Thomas Porter yells at the other man accompanying him.

While Thomas Porter is distracted, Willis ran out of the front doorway, and a truck's headlights blinded him as he exits. He shielded his eyes and then noticed that inside the truck was empty. Willis sprinted towards his SUV and spotted two more trucks speeding towards the barn. He quickly dashed into the tall grass next to him to plan his next move.

"Must be Porter's backup. Now, how am I going to get out of this? What was I thinking, getting involved in this?" Willis asked himself as he headed deeper into the prison grounds, with no other option.

As Willis moves quickly through the tall grass in the field into the prison grounds through the unfenced area, he tries again to send the images from his phone to Joy, but there is still no signal. Rather than give up, Willis decided to give a call, figuring that perhaps that would work if texting wouldn't. Quickly, Willis dialed 911, but the call immediately dropped.

"Come on!" Willis says in aggravation.

While hiding in the tall grass, Willis looks over at the men searching around the area for him with flashlights. He sees an opening in a broken fence area into the state hospital grounds area of the prison. Knowing he doesn't have long until Porter's men start searching in his direction in the field, Willis runs as fast as possible across the broken fence into the prison grounds.

"I never thought I would feel safer inside a prison than outside of it," Willis tells himself as he surveys the state hospital grounds, with its enormous old brick buildings surrounding him and the prison facility in the distance in front of him.

Willis wondered how far Thomas Porter's influence extended in the prison system. He also wondered how determined Porter would be to track him down. Fortunately, Willis had spent hours studying the blueprints of the Newberry State Hospital with Ted and by himself. He hoped that his knowledge would prove useful soon, as he urgently needed to find a place to hide.

Willis looked back at the barn. Porter's men were searching the tall grass fields where he had been moments ago. He saw the theater building ahead, where Ted used to spend the years of his childhood. Willis headed towards the theater. As he neared it, he noticed the open left entrance door. He slipped inside, using the prison's light to navigate.

As Willis enters the theater building, he notices how the auditorium looks just like Ted described it in his stories. On the main floor, there is a big stage with hundreds of wooden seats. There is also a balcony that Ted used to watch the performances from. The auditorium must have been a special place in its time. Willis walks down the center aisle. He steps through old party hats, stringers, and confetti. These are leftovers from the last event before it closed in the early 1990s. It feels as if time has stood still.

After a few seconds, Willis stops looking around the room. He focuses on finding a place to hide out. He glances up at the balcony, about which Ted has told him tales from his early years. The balcony looks like it could collapse after sitting empty for decades and undergoing erosion. If anyone comes looking for him, he could get trapped if he hides up in the balcony. It's better to find something on the main floor. Willis walks towards the large stage. The projector screen is still down and held together loosely by bits and pieces of the screen. Willis moves near the walls beside the large windows that face the stage. He glances at his phone battery and realizes it is quickly draining. He tries again to send his images or text to Joy, but there's still no signal. Willis sees some large stage props on the stage. Willis moves towards the stage props that should hide him until he can devise a secure an escape plan and find a signal to distribute the photos of the evidence.

As Willis sits alone in a dark corner of the stage, all he can do is think about the decisions that have led him to this point.

"How did it come to this?" Willis asks himself. "I should've just gone to the fireworks; what was I thinking? Trapped in the middle of the prison grounds, how am I going to escape?"

Willis thought about where he was in Newberry and what was close by.

He checked his phone and saw that it had only five percent battery left. Without a phone signal soon, finding the truth and evidence would be difficult. He remembered a gas station across the street from the prison where Joy used to make calls. It was one of the few places in town with a signal. Because of his concern that Porter's men might be waiting outside the prison, Willis was hesitant to run there. He weighed the risk of spending the night in the theater, turning off his phone, or making a run for it. Willis decides that staying put might be the best option. As he leaned against a stage prop, Willis thought about Joy and Ted and imagined how they must be feeling after his hours of absence.

Willis contemplated his options, weighing the risks and rewards of each. Finally, he was going to make a run for the gas station. He moved, but then he saw something that made him stop. There was a flashlight outside the theater building, shining through the glass windows.

"This could just be a regular prison patrol making their rounds. Don't overthink it," Willis tells himself.

Willis watches as the flashlight goes by the building, seeing the light come through the windows above him. It moves on in the distance, appearing to be a guard patrolling the rest of the prison grounds. After waiting for a few minutes, Willis moved towards the exit of the building. He stopped before opening the side door and tried to send the images one last time. His phone still had no signal, and now it only has three percent battery life left. Willis was about to shut off his phone when he heard the front door being pushed against from the outside. Willis rushed to the stage and hid behind a piano and some large stage props. He could look through the staging and see the two men who had pushed open the front door. The first man was a correctional officer, but Willis didn't recognize him. The second man was Thomas Porter.

"You're skilled at this cat-and-mouse game, boy; I'll give you that. But you need to understand that I run this town and this prison. It's time to give up. Nowhere else to run," Thomas Porter stated, holding a gun with a prison guard by his side. "Let's talk it out, like men. What do you say?"

Willis remained silent, watching from behind the stage piano. He gripped his large kitchen knife tightly. The door creaked open, revealing Thomas Porter. He wasn't alone. A prison guard stood beside him, both figures silhouetted against the hallway light. Porter gripped a gun tightly in his hand. The guard headed towards the balcony steps, stating, "I'll go up there and investigate."

"Sorry for what I said earlier about your wife, Willis. I was just messing with you," Thomas Porter says while looking around the main floor for Willis.

With his battery extremely low, Willis still decides to turn on the audio recorder app on his phone. Willis does this just in case someone finds the phone. He wants them to know what happened if he doesn't make it out alive.

"We could have ruled this town together. Boy, you remind me so much of myself. It's a shame we got off the wrong foot. You've become such a pest to me since you came to town. If you had just stayed in your lane, we wouldn't be here now. Mother Mary was easy to set up with her past, but you just wouldn't stop digging around, and now you're going to have to pay. "I am not one for loose ends, but if you all just follow the rules, I do not have to kill people or blow things up. Look at what I did to Sarah and her annoying boyfriend, Noah." Thomas Porter yells as he moves around the auditorium, frustrated that he cannot find Willis.

With his heart racing, Willis looks down at his phone, still recording at two percent battery life.

"How about, out of the goodness of my heart, I give you one last chance to repent of your sins and just come out?" Thomas asked, arming his handgun.

Thomas Porter glanced up at the balcony. The prison guard's flashlight scanned the area, but he couldn't locate Willis. Willis muttered to himself, desperately attempting to send the pictures from his phone. Frustration consumed him as the images refused to transmit. As Thomas Porter got closer and closer, Willis felt a wave of anxiety.

"All those people didn't have to die over the years, but they just couldn't follow the rules and had to be punished for their actions. You follow the rules or pay a heavy toll."

Thomas Porter continued to talk, searching for Willis. Willis looks around the stage behind him for an exit, but fallen scaffolding blocks the only exit.

"Those news stations sure made up a fun nickname for that guy we sent over to the Dirty Elk, the Gould City Killer. That idiot was just a drug addict willing to do anything for his next hit, collateral damage after he served his purpose. My favorite moment though was watching that prison guards house explode after he started asking too many questions. Maybe I should do the same thing with your building, Willis."

Porter abruptly stopped moving and speaking, scanning the area for any movement. The room was dead silent. A group of birds flapping their wings as they flew out the theater building's open front door was the only sound audible. Porter pulled his gun, startled. The stage area was the last place he had not yet checked, so he headed there. Perched on the balcony, the prison guard was aiming his firearm at the stage while glancing through the scope.

"Here's the thing, Willis. For generations, my family has kept this town safe. Every couple of years, someone like you comes around and tries messing with what we've built around here. Killing Sarah and the others was what I needed to do to restore fear to the community. Fear is a powerful tool. I bet you're feeling fear right now. Is there anything you want me to tell your son?" Thomas Porter asks, trying to get Willis to speak.

Thomas Porter hears something upstairs on the opposite side of the balcony from the guard, who signals him to check it out. With his gun drawn, Thomas Porter approaches the stage as the guard crosses to the other side of the large balcony and scans his surroundings. Willis can see Porter's silhouette on the screen in front of him. The quiet was broken only by the insistent buzz of Willis's phone. It vibrated violently in his hand, followed by a single, amplified ping that seemed to echo from the very walls themselves.

Looking down, Willis notices that Joy has finally received the images along with a confirmation message sent below the pictures of the evidence. He realizes that his phone somehow received enough signal to send the images. However, shortly afterward, his phone battery completely died. From the echoing ping across the auditorium, Willis realizes that now the prison guard and Thomas Porter know exactly where he's at.

"Now you've done it, kid. I'm going to have to kill anyone I know who's connected to you, Willis. This is way bigger than you think. By poking your nose into other people's affairs, you have pissed off the drug rings in Chicago and Detroit. Maybe I need to send them both a piece or two of you to get back on their good sides."

Porter moves towards Willis on the stage with his gun drawn, ready to fire at first sight of Willis.

"Whatever you just sent won't ever end up in the light of day. No one close to you will make it through the night. I'm going to enjoy throwing your lifeless body into Lake Superior. My forefathers will be proud of me for protecting our family name you tried to destroy," Thomas Porter says, moving closer to the end of the stage props, with Willis hidden behind them.

Thomas Porter aims his flashlight at Willis. Willis is crouched near a stage prop, trying to defend himself. He knows he's outmatched, armed only with a kitchen knife. As Porter turns in his direction, Willis thinks about Joy's smile and hopes his son will be proud of him for standing up for what's right. He knows he's about to die, but he believes the truth will eventually reach those who need it.

As Thomas Porter turned in Willis' direction, the sound of a gunshot rang out from the back of the theater building. It was not from the gun of Thomas Porter or the prison guard who fell with a thud from the balcony railing to the main floor.

Willis heard a second gunshot and dove covering his head. Lost in the moment, Willis didn't know if someone had shot him or if the adrenaline rushing through his veins was causing his heart to pound. When he looked up, Porter was staring right at him, his gun falling from his hand and his body collapsing to the floor. With a bullet hole squared between them, Willis was staring into the dead eyes of Thomas Porter. Blood slowly dripped from his forehead onto the wooden floor. Willis said nothing. He just stared at Porter, his eyes cold and lifeless.

Slowly, Willis stands up and walks to the other side of the stage to see who shot Thomas Porter and the prison guard. As Willis walks past the stage props, he sees Ted standing on the balcony with his rifle in his hand, looking down at Willis.

"Are you okay?" Ted yells down from the balcony.

"I'm better than okay. Thank you, Ted," Willis replies.

"I can't hear you," Ted shouted, cupping his hand over his ear and making a face to show that he couldn't understand Willis' words.

"Thank you!" Willis shouts to Ted.

"I heard you clearly the first time. I'll be right down," Ted says with a chuckle.

Upon exiting the stage, Willis turns to face Thomas Porter, who is motionless on the ground, his blood streaming down the stage to the theater room floor.

"I never killed a man, Willis, but if I had to kill a man, those two would be the ones," Ted says, walking towards Willis down the aisle in the auditorium.

"How did you find me and get in here?" Standing in the aisle next to Ted, Willis asks.

"You were right about Joy. She saw right through me, so I told her I would follow you and ensure you were fine. I didn't know where you were until I saw Porter coming into the prison grounds."

"How did you get up to the balcony?" Willis asks.

"I remember this place like it was yesterday. Sorry about the mess with Porter almost falling on top of you. I didn't mean to make such a mess with him. It's been years since I fired this gun. After all these years of not firing much, I'm a little rusty. I was aiming for his chest Porter's words left me reeling. The things he was saying were unspeakable.

"He really enjoys talking a lot."

"I can't say this enough; thank you," Willis says, reaching over and hugging Ted.

"I bet it shocked you to discover that I was the one up on the balcony," Ted replies.

"I'm just glad I didn't take your gun like you recommended. You saved my life," Willis says with a smile.

"All I can say is that the big man upstairs works in mysterious ways," Ted responds.

Willis and Ted heard police sirens as they talked. They stepped towards the front door with their hands in the air to turn themselves in. As Willis opened the front door, the upset agents stormed the room around him and Ted, paying no attention to them. Willis and Ted dropped to the floor, still expecting to be arrested. However, the agents ignored them and searched the theater building. Neal was the last of his team to arrive and approached Willis.

"Are you both okay?" Neal asks, putting his hand on Willis's shoulder.

"Still in shock, but I think we're fine," Willis answers, being helped up by Neal and another agent helping Ted to his feet.

"My unit got word that something was happening next to the prison. A resident reported hearing gunfire emanating from the prison. Then my wife and others started spreading the images you took all over social media. That took some serious balls going the length you did to get those images."

As they walked down the front steps of the theatre building, Willis looked off in the distance and saw police lights over at the barn area.

"We saw a group of Thomas Porter's guys running around with flashlights near the barn. Some of them ran inside the barn to destroy evidence by setting it on fire. However, we stopped them before they could cause any serious damage. One of his men, driving a timber-loaded semi-truck from downstate, tried to escape the state police by racing across Cut River Bridge. The truck lost control and flipped over, partially hanging off the railing, causing a big mess on the bridge and below. We soon had his location from two of Porter's men in the barn. We rushed over here, but it seems like you both already handled the situation," Neal explains, as more agents and state police officers raced around them into the theater building.

"My phone is dead, but I hit record on my audio recording app right before Thomas Porter started confessing to the murders and the drug ring," Willis shares.

"I can't believe I didn't see this coming with Thomas Porter. I guess I was too close to it and wanted Mary to go down for it anyway. Joy's online sharing left my wife horrified and in tears. Alice is showing the Michigan State Police and some agents through the offices right now. My wife is heartbroken over all the harm her father caused to her friends and the community she loves," Neal says while glancing through the doorway. Thomas Porter was on the stage. The agents were busy taking pictures of his lifeless body.

"I can only imagine what she's going through," Ted says to Neal.

"I'll tell my wife about her father's death once we're done here. I never liked the guy, but I loved her, so I managed. Thanks for not giving up on finding the truth. Maybe you'll have a job with us someday, Willis. Did you shoot them?" Neal asks.

"No, it was Ted here who shot them both from the balcony." Pointing at Ted, Willis answers.

"That's quite the aim, Mr. Jokela," Neal says.

"You can just call me Ted. I was just watching out for my family," Ted responds, looking over at Willis proudly.

"By the way, I overheard on the radio that there are some important people waiting for both of you outside the prison grounds. The state police and my agents will want

225

to ask both of you some questions later, but you can go see your family now." Neal shares.

Willis and Ted started walking towards the road, where they saw Joy, Archer, and Ruth waiting patiently. They were waving and smiling as Willis and Ted approached. Willis and Ted walked across the state hospital's broken front fence, and Joy and Archer ran over to hug Willis. Ted was hugged warmly by Ruth as well.

"I don't know if I want to slap or kiss you," Joy says, looking up at Willis as she hugs him, with Archer hugging his leg.

"I'll take a kiss first, but I deserve the slap. I've never been more happy to see you both in my entire life. I love you both so much," Willis says with a smile, getting a kiss from Joy.

"Can I get one of those?" Ted says, looking at Ruth after seeing Joy kiss Willis.

Ruth reaches up, cups Ted's face with both hands, and gives him a long, passionate kiss.

Willis and Ted reunited with their family, and in the distance, vibrant fireworks burst in the night sky. A frenzy of crackling erupted, and the unmistakable scent of gunpowder ignited one after another, creating a breathtaking display of color. Willis stood mesmerized, holding his son Archer and feeling Joy's love embrace him. Ted and Ruth watched in awe as the sky filled with this awe-inspiring spectacle. A sense of hope washed over Willis, soothing his soul like a gentle tide. The darkness that had shrouded Newberry disappeared, leaving behind a profound sense of peace. It felt as if Willis had returned to God's country, just like his first visit to Tahquamenon Falls years ago.

CHAPTER 37

There were weeks of uncertainty after Thomas Porter's death and the dissolution of the drug ring. The repercussions were felt throughout Newberry Village. Many generations of Porters were arrested as a result of additional information that the public provided to the authorities. Alice, Thomas Porter's daughter, changed the lumberyard's name from Porter Hughes Lumber to Hughes Lumber, reflecting the changing times. Other local businesses followed suit by removing "Porter" from their names too.

Ted and Willis were asked to testify by the court during the hearing. They provided valuable evidence and testimony. The court cleared Mary of all charges and released her to spend her last days with her grandchildren and children. Despite not being forgiven for her past actions, many in the village gave Mary a second chance. She spent her remaining days with her family, visiting her son Ethan in prison.

Larry was still recovering, his body gradually reawakening as he painstakingly regained control over his movements. Every small twitch and tremor felt like a victory, a step closer to reclaiming his lost abilities. The local logging community heard about his Woodhenge vision and donated funds to build it. Law enforcement brought down the drug rings across the Upper Peninsula of Michigan, and those involved in the rings provided information to help crack down on other drug rings across Michigan, Wisconsin, Illinois, and parts of Ontario.

Considering all that had transpired, Willis gave Chelsea full control of the Northern Bites for the upcoming season. Law enforcement and the FBI continued their crackdown across the Great Lakes region. As a result, Willis's family moved to an undisclosed location downstate, away from the investigation for now.

The FBI moved Willis and his family to a safe house outside Traverse City. Willis and his family spent months adapting to their new way of life, uncertain about how long they would live in their safe home. Even though Traverse City was only three hours away from Newberry, it felt like a completely different world. From his dining room table, Willis admired the scenic view of Elk Lake through the window. Willis opened his laptop and saw an email from Ted.

Willis, we did something special for this village. I can see the impact every day. The streets and yards are cleaner, and people around the village have more smiles on their faces. I might even start leaving my truck unlocked when I go grocery shopping next time. Chelsea is doing a fantastic job running Northern Bites while you're away. I visit from time to time to check on your building. Chelsea told me that Ava is doing well now, living on the reservation, as the tribal members are supporting her with love. Chelsea and her mother made Ava a necklace with Sarah's engagement ring that was found at the fire in Paradise. Ava wears the necklace all the time because it makes her feel more connected to her mother. I brought flowers to the cemetery for you to place on Noah and Sarah's gravestones. Can you believe it's almost been a year since they passed away? Time really needs to slow down.

Parts of this village are coming back to life. The grass looks greener, and the trees seem somehow even more beautiful than before. Over the past few decades, Newberry has become a shadow of its former self, bound by the chains of the past and existing only as a hollow shell. There are myths and there are truths. Now, Newberry's future seems endless. Though things are going great, we all miss you all here greatly. Your father would be proud of you, Willis. I know I sure am.
But now, the village is alive and free.

Thank you for not giving up on us and helping bring the truth to light. I look forward to seeing all of you when you can.
That's the latest.
Ted.

CHAPTER 38

Willis and his family were trying to return to a more normal life away from Newberry in the Grand Traverse area. They took a day trip to Sleeping Bear Dunes National Lakeshore, where they hiked on the sand dunes and planned to watch the sunset over Lake Michigan. Soaking in the sun on the dunes, Willis felt a vibration intrude on his peaceful moment. His new phone, issued by the secret service, rarely buzzed, making the sudden movement all the more intriguing. He took his phone out and saw that it was a text message from a number he didn't have saved on his phone. The message said:

Hello, my name is Lisa Russo. I hope this message reaches you. Ted, your father-in-law, gave me your phone number. My father vanished on Mackinac Island a few weeks ago, and I am asking for your assistance in finding him because I do not know where else to look. Everybody else has given up trying to locate him. I thought maybe you could help me find out what happened to my father after hearing about your actions on behalf of the missing people in Newberry and reading your story on the news. I know it may not seem appealing to get involved in the case of another missing person. But hopefully, you can assist us. Without your help, I don't know where else to turn.

Willis looked up at the setting sun, remembering the moment of being with Larry in his backyard labyrinth. He vividly remembered the moment he selflessly assisted Larry when everyone else hesitated. His father's unwavering advice echoed in his mind, urging him to persist and uncover the hidden layers of any situation. With the sun cascading its warm golden glow, Willis gazed out one last time and then replied to the text message.

I can help. Let's talk tomorrow.

Acknowledgements

I would like to express my sincere gratitude to the following people who helped make this book possible: My beautiful wife, Rebecca, for her love, patience, and support. Your hours of letting me escape to write brought this book to life. My son, Hayden, thank you for inspiring the character Archer with your wild creativity. I am so proud to be your father, and I loved those years with you as a little boy and my adventure buddy. My parents, Gary and Debbie, for letting me be myself and never pushing me in any other direction than to follow my dreams. My father and mother-in-law, Don and Judy, proudly showed me around the Upper Peninsula for the very first time. You are both perfect examples of what makes a yooper so special. My family from Michigan, Washington, and Missouri, for pushing me to continue writing and, more importantly, finishing this book. Rachel and Eric, for sharing moments of living next to an Amish community over the years and getting to see it firsthand every time we visited. The residents of Newberry, Michigan, for the endless real-life characters that couldn't all fit in one book or even a full-book series. Josiah, Tim, Bob, Allen, Brian, Ed, and John, for your great conversations over the years running my coffee shop, Great Waters Coffee Company, inspired this book to happen. Doug Weaver and the team at Mission Point Press for helping me make this book so much stronger. My close friend, Anthony Kelly, from across the pond in Ireland, for your feedback on the early drafts and friendship. Karen Dionne and Ellen Airgood, best-selling authors, for taking time out of your busy days to help mentor me on the direction to go at the beginning of the book writing process to set me in the right direction. Jake Phillips, for your insight into the world of police investigation and undercover cop procedures to make my writing more realistic. The team at Pegasus and Vanguard Press for believing in this book.

I am truly grateful for your support and encouragement. This book would not have been possible without you.

Thank you.

About the Author

David Kenny is a seasoned creative with a restless spirit. For over two decades, he's balanced a successful career in professional photography with a passion for writing and design. His travels have taken him across all 50 states and countless corners of the globe, each new experience fueling his imagination. Now residing in Northern Michigan with his family, David continues to explore the world through his lens and translate those experiences into captivating stories.